*Ivy and
Allison*

Also by Jane Peart

Ivy and Allison

Jane Peart

Fleming H. Revell
A Division of Baker Book House Co
Grand Rapids, Michigan 49516

Published by Fleming H. Revell
a division of Baker Book House Company
P.O. Box 6287, Grand Rapids, MI 49516-6287

Adapted from *The Heart's Lonely Secret*, published in 1994

Printed in the United States of America

Library of Congress Cataloging-in-Publication Data
Peart, Jane.
   Ivy and Allison / Jane Peart.
       p. cm.—(Orphan train west)
   Abridged from: The heart's lonely secret.
   Summary: Ever since she was adopted at age eight, Ivy has carried secrets that affected the course of her life, causing grief as well as teaching trust in God.
   ISBN 0-8007-5714-9 (paper)
   [1. Orphans—Fiction. 2. Adoption—Fiction. 3. Secrets—Fiction. 4. Christian life—Fiction.] I. Peart, Jane. The heart's lonely secret. II. Title.
PZ7.P32335 Iv 2000
[Fic]—dc21   99-048425

Scripture quotations are from the King James Version of the Bible.

For current information about all releases from Baker Book House, visit our web site:
http://www.bakerbooks.com

Boston, 1884

Ivy bolted upright in her small white iron bed, not sure what had awakened her. Was it the rain beating on the tin roof over the slanted ceiling of her little bedroom? Or was it the sound of voices drifting up the narrow stairway? Did Mama and Papa have company?

Ivy decided to go see for herself. She would tiptoe down the stairs and peek over the railing to look into the kitchen. Sometimes when her papa came home late at night from his job as a fireman, her parents would sit at the table having tea and talking. She felt thirsty. She would ask for a drink of water.

Ivy was sure they wouldn't mind if she came down, even if she was supposed to be asleep. Papa would grin and pick her up and give her a hug. She could almost feel the roughness of his uniform jacket and the shiny brass buttons pressed against her cheek. Mama would pretend to be cross and shake her finger at Ivy playfully, saying, "No time for a five-year-old to be awake."

Ivy smiled to herself as she crept down the hallway in her bare feet, sure of a warm welcome and the secure love that had always surrounded her.

But it didn't happen as she expected. Halfway down the stairs she halted. She heard her mama crying over and over, "It can't be true! Will can't be dead!"

A man's deep voice said, "I'm so sorry, Mrs. Austin, but it is true. Please know that your husband died in the line of duty. He was a very brave man."

Died? What did that mean? Had something happened to Papa? Ivy felt cold and sick.

In the bleak days that followed, her mother cried all the time, and neighbors came and went in a dreary procession. Finally, Mama took to her bed, and a few weeks later, she, too, was gone.

Ivy wasn't sure how many days had passed when one of the neighbor women buttoned her into her winter coat, tied her bonnet strings under her chin, and took her by the hand, saying, "Come along, Ivy. I'm taking you to the orphanage."

"What's an orphanage?" Ivy's lower lip trembled.

"It's a place where they take care of children who have no mama or papa."

"To stay?"

"Yes, Ivy. You see, you're an orphan now."

Ivy felt very afraid. She didn't want to be an orphan. It sounded scary.

The day Ivy was left at Greystone Orphanage she knew her life would never be the same.

Greystone Orphanage, March 1887

The loud whistle split the chilly March air. Recreation time was over for the day, so the children straggled into line. The older ones gathered up balls and beanbags and jump ropes and deposited them in the large wood storage bins beside the playground fence. Ivy gave one longing glance over her shoulder at the chalked hopscotch layout on the cracked cement. She dreaded the hour ahead.

Quietly, the eight-year-old took her place in line with the rest of the children. At least today she would have to stay in study period only a few minutes. At five o'clock she had to report to the dining room. It was her turn to set the tables. Just as she walked inside, however, she felt a strong grip on her shoulder. It was Miss Preston, the hall monitor.

"Ivy, you're wanted in the front office. But first, go to your room and put your things in this." The woman thrust a small canvas suitcase toward her. "And brush your hair." She straightened the collar of Ivy's coarse cotton dress. "Now hurry!"

In the three years Ivy had been at Greystone, she had learned not to ask too many questions, so she scurried up the two flights of steps without a word. All the while her mind whirled like a jump rope. What was this all about? Was she going somewhere? A flutter of hope stirred in her small chest. Maybe, just maybe . . .

A few minutes later, Ivy knocked on the door of Miss Clinock's office.

"Come in," the head matron's voice directed.

The only times the children went into Miss Clinock's office were if they had done something bad or had broken one of the rules or were going somewhere. Ivy's heart skipped a beat. She stepped inside.

"Hello, Ivy. Shut the door please and take a seat," Miss Clinock said. To the dark-haired man sitting opposite her desk she asked, "Is this the child you meant?"

The man squinted at Ivy and nodded. His penetrating look made her shiver.

Miss Clinock bent over her desk, writing rapidly. Her pen scraping against a piece of paper was the only sound beside the ticking wall clock.

"Well, Mr. Tarantino, everything seems to be in order." The head matron placed the paper into a file folder with some other papers and handed it to the man. "Everything is signed. As I pointed out, since she has no living relatives, we have the authority to release her into your custody."

The stranger rolled up the folder and stuffed it into the side pocket of his plaid jacket.

Miss Clinock stood up. "Your agreement is to provide shelter, food, and an education through the eighth grade until she's fifteen." She looked at Ivy. "Ivy, this is Mr. Paulo Tarantino. He's adopting you."

Adopting! Ivy clutched her suitcase tightly and swallowed hard. She often imagined what it would be like to be adopted, to have a real home again. It felt like she had lived at Greystone all her life, and she was having more and more trouble remembering her real mother and father. The nightmares about the night her father had been killed and the day her mother had died still terrified her, but the youngster clung to them, terrified that without them she would forget her parents completely.

And now *she* was being adopted, like other children she had known. Her heart began to thump fast. What kind of family would it be? Were there other children? Where was their home?

Miss Clinock walked around the big desk, bent down, and tucked a tiny black New Testament into the pocket of Ivy's gray jacket. "Good-bye, Ivy," she said. "Be a good child and do as you're told."

Delivery carts, tram cars, and carriages crowded the bustling streets of Boston as their wagon rumbled along.

"You like animals?" the man suddenly asked. His words were as clipped as the sound of the horse and buggy passing by.

Ivy's dark, curly hair blew back in the breeze as she nodded.

He gave a short, harsh laugh. "Well, ya better. That's all I gotta say."

The youngster held on to the handle on the side of the wagon while it jostled along the rutted lanes just past the city limits.

As they rounded the corner, the little girl could hear the loud clatter of a train engine before she could see it. "Whoa!" the man cried as he pulled back on the reins.

The buggy stopped, and dust swirled around its wheels. The train whizzed by.

Something inside her heart quickened every time she heard a locomotive. The sound of the long line of train cars clamoring on the metal tracks made the hair on her head prickle. At Greystone, she had often heard the mournful wail through the open windows of the dormitory room at night. The sound was so sad, and it made her feel so lonely. She felt very alone now.

As the caboose passed and the clanging died down, Ivy looked across the tracks. She spotted a circle of colorful wagons with the words "Higgins Brothers' Circus" painted on their sides. Ivy had never seen a real circus before.

"Get'yup." The strange man clucked his tongue, and the wagon lurched forward.

To her surprise, it crossed the tracks and threaded its way through the maze of painted wagons, finally stopping in front of a small canvas tent.

"Hey, Angela!" His words were almost as loud as the train that had just passed. "I got the kid."

A moment later, a thin woman in a gaudy flowered robe pulled back the tent flap. Her dark shadowed eyes surveyed Ivy, and her full red lips curled unpleasantly. "I thought you wuz gettin' a boy!"

All of a sudden, the man started yelling at the woman in another language. Then he slapped the reins on the horse's back, and the wagon jerked forward again.

"You'll be sleepin' in Sophia's wagon," he muttered. "She used to be one of us, until she got too old and fat. Now she tells fortunes." The man's steely eyes bored into her. Ivy did not move. "But you take orders from me, ya hear?" He jabbed his finger toward her. "And nobody else!"

The frightened girl quickly nodded.

A few minutes later, he hitched the horse to a post near one of the big tents. "Come on," he barked.

Even though Mr. Tarantino wasn't very tall, Ivy's short legs had a hard time keeping up with him. All around her were webs of tangled ropes and yards of canvas. Men dressed in dirty work clothes were pulling and tugging and yelling. Some jugglers were tossing rings and dumbbells into the air while two men toted a deep cardboard box stuffed with pink and blue teddy bears.

"Hey, you kid, stop gawkin'!" Paulo yelled back at her.

Carrying her heavy suitcase, Ivy tried to hurry. Suddenly, a deafening roar startled her. Right beside her, the biggest tiger she had ever seen clawed at the bars of its cage. His jagged, shiny, white fangs snarled at her. Ivy stood there, rooted to the spot. She had followed Mr. Tarantino right into a nest of huge cages holding animals she had seen only in picture books. Her chest thumped so hard she thought it might explode.

"Come on. I ain't got all day!"

Shifting her suitcase to the other hand, the little girl scurried forward. At last Mr. Tarantino stopped in front of a brightly painted wagon decorated with clouds and stars and moons. He rapped on the little arched door.

"Sophia! You in there? It's Paulo."

"Whatcha want?" The door inched open, and a round moon of a face topped with fiery orange hair peeked out. Ivy had never seen hair that color. "Why, Paulo, she's a girl! I thought you wuz gettin' a boy."

Ivy took a step back.

Paulo shrugged his wide shoulders. "What's the difference? Can she sleep here tonight? We ain't got no room in the tent."

The woman hesitated.

"Well, can she?" He shifted back and forth from one foot to the other.

"All right," she grumbled.

Paulo stroked his chin. He looked satisfied. "You stay here tonight, kid. Tomorrow we'll start your trainin'— ridin' a horse. You'll like that. All kids like ponies." He rapped her head with his knuckles and walked off.

Ivy rubbed the spot on her head. It felt sore.

"Come on in, little lady."

She followed the big woman inside. The caravan was like a real-life dollhouse! Dainty ruffled white curtains hung at the tiny slatted windows. Colorful paper flowers filled green glass bottles and speckled pottery mugs. Costumed dolls adorned two wooden shelves, and pretty Japanese fans were tacked onto one wall. The little girl put down her suitcase and plopped down on the edge of a pillowed chair.

"You hungry?"

"Yes, ma'am," Ivy replied, sniffing the mouthwatering smell of beef stew. It was past supper time at Greystone.

She watched the heavyset woman stir the contents of a small iron pot with a wooden spoon. Her smile revealed lots of missing teeth, but her eyes were kind and her voice soothing.

"What's your name?"

"Ivy, Ivy Austin."

"Ivy? Well, Paulo will probably change it." She shrugged. "He'll make it something Italian, I'm sure. But it don't matter now, does it?" She ladled the thick stew into two bowls. "It's what's inside that counts." Sophia set the bowls on a small round table. "Right here," she tapped her chest with her finger. "Don't let them change you there, little lady."

After supper, Sophia helped her unpack some bedclothes.

"Time to turn in," she told her.

The caravan was warm and her stomach was full, and Ivy quickly drifted off to sleep. Maybe life at the circus wasn't going to be so bad after all.

3

When Ivy awoke the next morning, she eased herself up and out of the little bed of folded quilts and pillows Sophia had set up for her. The sound of snoring floated from behind the curtains at the far end of the wagon. The youngster quietly got dressed and tied her curly hair into a ponytail.

As she did, she noticed some bright orange hair resting on a wooden stand on top of a bureau. Why, that wasn't Sophia's real hair at all—it was a wig! Ivy wondered what other new things she would discover today.

Since Sophia had already told her about the cookhouse tent, Ivy ventured out to find it. She had taken only a few steps when she heard a cheery voice.

"Hello there. Lookin' for somebody?"

A bald-headed man with a weathered face and short brown beard approached her.

"You're new around here, ain't cha?" The man's blue eyes twinkled.

"I'm lookin' for the cookhouse," she said shyly, cocking her head to one side.

"It's breakfast you're wantin', is it? Well, come along then. I'm goin' there myself. You can tag along. My name's Timothy O'Brien, but ever'one calls me Gyppo."

"I'm Ivy Austin."

"That's a nice name. I'll bet a dollar to a doughnut you're with the Tarantinos."

The pair approached a large tent.

"How'd you know?"

"Not many secrets 'round here." Gyppo laughed. "Paulo and his two brothers had a fallin' out a while back. Luca and Tonio up and left. Didn't even show up for the last performance. Lots of us thought they'd cool off and come back. But they didn't."

"So what happened?"

"I guess *you* happened!" He smiled. "Paulo's been braggin' how he could replace 'em, no problem. Says he can train someone in three weeks. Talk's been he's been scoutin' around some orphanages, lookin'." Her new friend's smile showed big white teeth. "Time was gettin' short. The season's 'bout to open. I guess you're it, kid."

The smell of coffee and frying sausage wafted through the tent door. Ivy could feel her empty stomach growl. Gyppo held back the heavy canvas flap.

"You eat at the performers' table with me this mornin'," he told her.

Ivy could hardly believe it. A lady cook in a white apron loaded her tin plate with fluffy scrambled eggs and warm sausage links. She even added two strips of crispy bacon. This was certainly different from the breakfast of lumpy oatmeal and watery cocoa at Greystone.

A short while later, Ivy heard the loud angry voices of a man and woman approaching the tent. She looked around to see Paulo and the woman called Angela. His lips were snarling and his eyes glared. When he saw Ivy, he stomped toward the table but acted like he hadn't even seen her.

"Gyppo, can the kid hang 'round with you for a while? I got some things t'do and cain't get her horse yit."

Gyppo wiped his mouth with a blue-checkered napkin. "Glad t'have the company." He gave Ivy a broad wink. "How 'bout you and me goin' to see the elephants?"

"Oh yes!" Ivy replied, relieved that she didn't have to go off with Paulo right away.

Outside, the men were already working to set up the big top, the tent in which people would watch the main events.

"They do this nearly every day." Gyppo's bushy eyebrows moved up and down as he talked. "Each night, after the final performance, they take it all down and are ready to move on to the next town and set it all up again. But we're not due to start for another week. So this week the performers are puttin' the finishin' touches on their acts."

The sound of the elephants' loud shrill cries grew louder as they approached. Gyppo told her this noise was called trumpeting.

The animals were lined up just outside the camp. They were as big as whales and as tall as giraffes. Their skin was gray and wrinkled, and their ears flapped back and forth switching at flies. Two wore fancy feathered headdresses and gold-trimmed capes, while another munched on some stalks of hay. When Ivy's nose wrinkled at the smell, Gyppo laughed heartily. "This is the circus! You'll get used to it."

Just then Paulo suddenly appeared with a black and white pony behind him, shaking its dusty mane and twitching its nostrils.

"Come on, kid. Let's go," he said to Ivy.

"Thanks, Gyppo." Ivy waved as she left.

"Good luck, Ivy," Gyppo called out after her.

4

For all her fear, Ivy's first training session wasn't too bad. She learned how to mount the pony, place her feet in the metal stirrups, and hold the leather reins. As Paulo barked commands, the horse obediently walked and cantered around the circle. Paulo never looked directly at Ivy, and he spoke sharply every time he said anything.

When they finished, the man showed her how to get down. "Tomorrow we get down to business. You go back to Sophia's now." Paulo ran his short fingers through his black greasy hair, swiped the reins over the horse's pointed ears, and steered the animal out of the ring.

Ivy quickly realized she was on her own. The circus was so different from the orphanage, where every minute of every day the orphans were told what to do and how to do it. Like a bird that had escaped its cage, Ivy felt a new freedom.

She set out to find her way back to Sophia's as if she were on a hunt. She strolled along, shuffling the soles of her high-top shoes in the dry dirt. She wandered alone beside the tents, stepping over the ropes staked to the ground. She inched her way by the tiger's cage, holding her breath as if it might give her away. Finally she spotted the brightly painted wagon with a curved roof and painted scenes on its sides.

Relieved, Ivy skipped up to the bottom step. Just then, a large woman dressed in a rainbow-colored gown appeared in the doorway. She had a colorful scarf tied over her head. A tangle of shiny beads swung around her neck, and long, glittering earrings dangled from her ears. Two circles of thick red rouge dotted her fat cheeks, and her round eyes were lined in black pencil with purple eye shadow.

Ivy stared at the strange-looking lady. Then, she heard a deep familiar laugh. It was Sophia! She had been transformed into a gypsy.

"Scared you, did I?" she chuckled. "I'm sorry, love. It's me. Only now I'm Romany Rovina, the gypsy fortune-teller who knows all and tells all . . . for a price." Sophia held out her right hand. "Cross my palm with silver, little lady, and I'll tell you your past, present, and future." Then she paused. "Poor kid, I don't think I want t'know your future, with Paulo."

"Now, don't be worryin' her, Sophia," a lilting voice warned from behind. "Save your predictions for the 'towners.'"

Ivy spun around to see a white-powdered face sporting a huge painted grin and a nose that looked like a red ball. Yarn the color of straw sprouted from beneath a dented black top hat.

"Wanta go to the big top and watch the rehearsals, Ivy?" he asked. "It's the biggest tent of all."

"Oh yes!" she exclaimed happily, realizing at once it was Gyppo.

"Well, come along then. I'll give you a guided tour."

"Show her the midway too, where I'll be," thundered Sophia from the open door of her caravan.

"What's a midway?"

"The midway is where they sell hot dogs, balloons, and cotton candy. You can play darts and win stuffed animals. And of course there are the sideshows—"

"The freaks," Sophia chimed in.

Ivy let her jaw drop.

"Alligator man with skin like a reptile," the fortune-teller jabbered on, "the bearded lady, Martina the snake charmer, and of course Jojo, the tattooed man."

Ivy looked back and forth between the two grown-ups. She couldn't believe her ears. Freaks?

"It's a livin', ain't it?" Sophia asked, her bracelets jangling in the air. "If it weren't for the circus, what kind of job could they get? Who else would hire them?"

Ivy pursed her lips. She guessed Sophia was right. No one else would hire a bearded lady or a tattooed man. The little girl shuddered. She wasn't at all sure she wanted to visit the midway.

Gyppo tipped his hat politely and held out his hand to Ivy. When she took it, he squeezed hers and a loud horn blared. She jumped back in alarm then giggled. It had been a trick. Sophia joined in, and, pleased with himself, Gyppo roared with laughter.

As they entered the big top, the sounds of brass instruments filled the noisy arena. Sitting at ringside, Ivy soon learned a great deal about the circus. She watched a sheik in a gold turban and beaded vest crack a long whip at roaring tigers who were hopping back and forth through flaming hoops inside a wire cage. A tall skinny man with the longest legs Ivy had ever seen walked in front of the ring, looking as if he could touch the sky. A stilt walker!

At one point, Ivy recognized the woman who had been arguing with Paulo. Angela. Dressed in a green satin costume, Angela leaped onto a horse's back and waved at the pretend audience. Paulo's whip kept the magnificent white horse cantering around the ring while the lady performed dangerous acrobatic stunts. Ivy crossed both her index fingers. Did Paulo expect her to do that?

Then, Ivy's attention riveted on the trapezes suspended so high in the air they were almost invisible.

"Gyppo, who're they?" Ivy gulped.

"They're the Flying Fortunatos." Gyppo put his finger to his lips to signal Ivy to be quiet.

Delicately perched on a high platform was a blond lady in a pink leotard and tights. She was pushing one of the swings toward a man who was already swaying back and forth in the air on another trapeze.

As she watched, the man slipped down to his knees, hung upside down, and crossed himself with a sign of the cross. Then the slender blond woman grabbed her bar and swooshed into the air, swaying back and forth like the pendulum on a clock. When the girl released her swing and leaped through the air toward the man, Ivy's stomach felt as if it had crawled up into her throat.

How could these people do this? Ivy wondered as her heart pounded like a hammer. They were flying in the air with only a flimsy net to catch them!

Everyone remained quiet until the performer finally reached the safety of the platform at the opposite side.

After two curtsies, she clambered down the rope ladder to the net, scrambled across, and flipped herself over the edge onto the hard ground below.

"Magnificent, Liselle!" Gyppo applauded.

"Merci!" The pretty lady breathed heavily as she bounded toward them. "And who's your little friend?"

The acrobat's voice sounded like music.

"This is Ivy." Gyppo bowed down toward the little girl, the toes of his big shoes pointing out. "She's one of us now, Tarantino's new act."

The rosebud mouth curved down. *"Ah, mais non!"*

"Yup, 'fraid so."

"Well, Ivy, welcome to the circus." Liselle offered her a hand.

"I don't know how you do that!" Ivy exclaimed.

The pretty woman smiled. "I started young. It just takes lots of practice, that's all." A dimple indented each cheek. "I follow two main rules—don't look down and don't panic. God will take care of the rest."

The words struck Ivy as if they had been a rock in a slingshot. Somehow, she was going to need these rules. She determined to remember them.

"Would you like to try sometime, *cherie?*" Liselle's eyes twinkled merrily.

Ivy cocked her head to one side as she tried to decide.

"I can show you. Who knows, you might like it better than riding the horse!"

5

Paulo banged on Sophia's door early the next morning. He took Ivy directly to the Tarantino tent and shoved her inside.

"But Paulo, it's so pretty!" Angela protested, slipping her fingers through Ivy's silky brown curls.

"Cut it!" he shouted. "We can't bill her as 'the Boy Wonder' if she has long curls."

With a towel pinned around her shoulders, Ivy sat quietly, watching her dark spirals fall one by one to the floor. The scissors finally stopped snipping. When Angela gave her a mirror, the little girl's heart sank. She looked like somebody else.

"You'll get used to it." The woman shrugged.

Ivy didn't have much time to dwell on her appearance though. She was too busy learning to ride. Every day for the next month Paulo had her practice on the vacant lot near the outside wagons. From morning to afternoon, she bounced in the saddle, trying to keep her feet from slipping out of the stirrups. With each jog, her neck wrenched and the leather reins cut into her tender hands. She bit her lip to keep from crying. Around and around she went until Paulo would finally yell, "Whoa!"

Practice, practice, and more practice became the order of Ivy's days. Sometimes she was too tired to eat the supper Sophia had made for her. Frequently, Sophia boiled water and poured it into a tub to soothe Ivy's twitching muscles. When Ivy tried to sleep at night, her ears would ring with the sound of Paulo's harsh commands.

"Paulo, the kid needs some time off!" Angela pleaded one day beside the ring. "You can't have her practicing all the time."

"Who asked you?" He cracked his knuckles at her. "I'm running this act, and I'll make the decisions."

If it hadn't been for school, Ivy would have been working seven days a week. However, since the circus season ran from May through October, the children took classes on Sundays. Martina, the lady snake charmer, taught them. Ivy looked forward to each Sunday. It was her only day off.

One morning, Paulo announced she was going to learn a new trick. "Soon you'll be in the act." His steely eyes sparked fire. "Now git up. I'm gonna teach ya the lean back."

To perform this trick, Ivy had to hold on to a special handle on the saddle. With one hand, she had to bend as far back as possible, and then she had to wave at the crowd with her free hand.

"Lean back! Lean back!" Paulo ordered. "Take your hand off the reins, wave to the crowd, and smile!"

For some reason, Ivy's pony, Mitzi, kept rearing up. Finally, Paulo grabbed the reins and pulled Mitzi to a stop. Then he yanked Ivy off the pony.

"You stupid kid, don't you understand?".

At that moment, he slapped her across her face so hard her head snapped back.

"Now get back on and do it again!" he shouted.

That afternoon, the little girl flung herself on Sophia's flowered couch and buried her sobbing face in one of the blue pillows.

"I hate the circus!" she cried. "I hate horses! When I grow up I never want to ride again."

"Once you're performing and you hear the crowd applaud, you'll feel differently," Sophia told her. "Once you get sawdust in your blood, dearie, you never get it out."

Ivy raised her head. "Well, *I* will!" she replied defiantly. "I *will!*"

The following morning, Ivy visited Liselle in her large wagon with the name *Fortunato* painted in curved letters on each side. The little girl's cheek was so swollen it looked like she had crammed it full of cloth.

"What happened, little one?" Sympathy softened Liselle's French accent.

The acrobat placed a worn Bible on her dressing table. Getting up from her chair, she walked over to touch the child's face ever so gently.

"Don't tell me," she said. "Paulo."

From then on, Liselle often accompanied Ivy to her practice sessions, showing Paulo that someone was watching out for her. Ivy thought Liselle was the most beautiful person she had ever known.

6

By March 1888, Ivy was a full-fledged member of the act. The circus billed her as "the Boy Wonder." They traveled hundreds of miles and played in dozens of small towns.

Although she hated pretending to be a boy, Ivy began to feel at home with her friends Sophia, Gyppo, and Liselle. When the circus wagons rumbled through a small town, Ivy watched children playing in their yards and mothers rocking their babies on the front porches. She wondered what it would be like to live that way. But Sophia would bustle around the caravan saying things like, "Life isn't so bad here, is it? Why, many children dream of belonging to a circus. And *you* are here!"

Frequently, after the evening performance, Ivy met Sophia at her booth on the midway, and the two walked back to the caravan together.

"Can you really see into the future with your crystal ball?" she asked Sophia as they walked back to the wagon one evening. Sophia shook her bright orange hair. "Nobody can see into the future, little one. And if they could, they wouldn't want to."

Sometimes Sophia was silent when they were together. Ivy came to understand that Sophia missed performing with the Tarantinos. The fortune-teller had once been an accomplished horsewoman. Giving up the roar of the crowd as she galloped into the big top had been hard for the aging gypsy. At these times, Ivy kept quiet, and soon Sophia would be her old self again.

Gyppo remained her best friend. The kindly clown would let her perch on the front seat of his wagon when he rode ahead of the circus. One of his jobs was to post cardboard arrows on lampposts and fences directing the townspeople to the performances. She always enjoyed being with him.

Ivy thought Liselle Fortunato was the bravest person she had ever known. Frequently, the child would hover near the huge net to watch the family practice. Each member would cross himself before grabbing the trapeze. Then, over and over they would tumble into each other's hands, swirling in the air like graceful doves. It was magical.

One afternoon, the performer spotted her young friend.

"Would you like to try today, *mon ami?* I'm going to work on my tightrope walking." Liselle brushed some sawdust off the bottom of one of her pink ballet slippers.

Ivy reluctantly agreed. She mounted the swaying rope ladder with her friend, grabbing each band and holding on tightly. As she crawled up toward the platform she looked up. The ropes and poles along the top of the tent had suddenly tripled in size.

As soon as Liselle mounted the platform, she reached back for Ivy. But the little girl was peering below.

"Oh, Liselle." Ivy had to catch her breath. "It's high up here! They look like tiny ants down there." Ivy had just scaled the last step.

Liselle reached out for her. "Everyone's scared at first, *cherie*. But you must learn never to look down! And if you feel frightened, you stop, say a little prayer, take a deep breath, and go on."

The feeling of safety from Liselle's hands didn't last. The first time Ivy's big toe touched the thin wire, she knew she didn't want to do this.

"I'll hold you," Liselle promised.

"I don't want to do it, Liselle." Ivy's brown eyes pleaded. "Please, I feel like I'm going to fall."

Ivy never did walk the tightrope, and the uncomfortable memory of climbing so high would haunt her for years to come.

By the fall of 1888, Ivy had learned dozens of tricks. But this wasn't enough for Paulo. He kept trying to teach her new ones. One particular lean back trick was giving her a great deal of trouble. Over and over they practiced until Ivy's hands were crusted with blisters.

One chilly morning, Ivy awoke to the smell of rain. She quickly slipped down the steps of Sophia's wagon, now sunk up to its hubs. The circus had just arrived in a new town, and the lot had turned into one huge slimy brown lake overnight. Gingerly, she jumped over puddles and sloshed through the mud toward the cookhouse tent.

All around her, workers shouted as they struggled to unroll the wet canvas for the big top. She wondered if anyone would really come out in this weather to attend the show.

"Good morning, *ma petite*. How are you?" Liselle set her breakfast tray down beside Ivy. "How's your new trick?"

"I still don't have it, and Paulo gets so mad."

No sooner had she spoken his name than he strutted into the tent. With his hands in his pockets, Paulo tromped over to Ivy. "We do the trick tonight," he said casually but firmly.

Ivy nodded. Paulo spun on his heels and went to get breakfast.

That afternoon, Ivy ran through the steps of the act in her mind. She was supposed to run beside Mitzi. On the fourth round, she was supposed to jump onto the pony's back in a flying leap-mount. At this point, she had to stand up and circle five more times. Although she didn't feel easy about it yet, Ivy was determined to try.

She got into her Spanish-style costume early so she could stop by the horse tent to give Mitzi a few sugar lumps from breakfast. The squishy ground left wet mud marks around the edges of her shiny boots. As she entered the large tent, she stomped her feet on the damp ground.

"Howdy, Ivy." It was Jojo, the tattooed man. Like most of the circus performers, he had other jobs too. One was shoveling hay. The man's cheery voice helped calm Ivy's nerves. "Bad weather ain't it?"

In the past year and a half, Ivy had learned that the "freaks" along the midway were really just people like herself. Sometimes their looks bothered her, but they acted normal, and they were nice to her.

"I thought I'd visit Mitzi before the show, Jojo." Ivy walked toward her pony's stall. "Have you seen anyone spreading sawdust in the ring this morning?" she asked.

"Nope, cain't say I has," Jojo replied. "Hope they do, though. Wouldn't want to see yer horse slide on the slippery ground, little lady."

Ivy nodded her head in agreement as Mitzi's cool nose nuzzled her hand for the sweet-smelling treat.

At last, the afternoon show began. Ivy heard the band music marking her entrance. Mitzi's ears twitched as she mounted. She could feel the pony's flanks quivering beneath her. Ivy patted the horse's right shoulder, rubbing its short hair.

Ivy took a deep breath, clucked her tongue, and galloped into the tent. As she circled the ring, the music grew louder. The applause surrounded her. Then all of a sudden, a loud popping sound blasted the arena. In a flash, Mitzi balked. The frightened pony lowered her head, and her body instantly slid across the slick sawdust.

Before Ivy knew what was happening, her hand had lost its grip on the saddle horn and her body was sailing over the pony's head toward the ring's metal rim. The last thing she remembered was a sharp blow to her head and the awful cracking sound of her leg.

7

Ivy ran her tongue along her parched lips and tried to swallow. Her head felt as if someone had twisted a tight metal band around it and was still squeezing. Her left leg throbbed fiercely.

The stabbing pain behind her eyes forced her to squint in order to see. Gradually, objects swam into focus. A high window let in filtered sunlight, while a white curtain sealed in her narrow bed.

A small moan escaped as she tried to push herself up. She heard a rustle beside her and a face framed in a starched, white-winged cap came into view.

"So we're awake, are we?" the rosy-cheeked face asked. "And how're we feelin'?"

"I'm thirsty," Ivy croaked in a voice she hardly recognized as her own.

"Here, take a sip of water then."

The lady nurse gently inserted a glass tube between Ivy's dry lips.

"Does your head hurt?"

Ivy tried to nod but couldn't.

"There now, don't try to move. You've a bit of a concussion. Took a bad fall, you did. Your leg's broke, all splinted up. You'll be staying put for a while, so you might as well get used to it."

Slowly, it all came back. Racing around the ring. Mitzi's slide. The agony of the pain.

"But I can't—"

"Oh yes you can." The nurse padded silently to the other side of the bed to tuck in the sheet. "We'll be takin' good care of you here at St. Luke's."

For the next four weeks, Nurse Halloran cared for Ivy like a baby. Hospital volunteers entertained her and the other children with puppet shows and music. Ivy really enjoyed herself.

"Why haven't any of the circus folks been to see me?" Ivy asked the nurse one morning while practicing with her crutches.

"Never you mind," Nurse Halloran replied briskly as she picked up the breakfast tray. "It'll all work out."

As Ivy hobbled around the room, she thought about Paulo and Sophia and Gyppo and Liselle. The circus had shows to put on; it couldn't wait for Ivy to get better. It was already October, and soon the circus would be heading south for the winter. She wondered who Paulo would send to get her now that she was almost completely well and ready to leave the hospital.

A couple of days later, Ivy decided to visit some patients down the hallway. As she hobbled out of the children's ward, she overheard Nurse Halloran chatting with another nurse.

"It's a terrible shame," Nurse Halloran was saying. "What kind of people would abandon a poor little girl in a hospital?"

"Well, what can we do?" the other nurse asked. "The doctor thinks we'll have to place her at the orphanage."

"I have an idea, but I need to check it out." It was Nurse Halloran again. "A missionary recently visited my sister's church and is taking orphans to communities in the West to place them in Christian families."

Ivy turned and hopped as fast as she could back down the hallway. She felt hot, then cold. They had been talking about her! Paulo *wasn't* coming for her or sending anyone for her. That was the awful truth.

She wondered about her three circus friends. Had they left her too? Where were they now? While the nightmares didn't come as often anymore, she still remembered her papa and mama. They had been taken away from her. And she had gone to live at Greystone. Ivy thought about the children, the gray uniforms, the high wire fence. She never wanted to go to a place like that ever again! No, she wanted a family, a real father and mother. She longed to be loved, to belong. Yet, here she was alone again. Abandoned.

Ivy had kept the small New Testament Miss Clinock had given her. She pulled it out from under her pillow and looked at the picture of Jesus inside the front cover. He was surrounded by little children. Underneath was the quotation, "Suffer the little children to come unto me, and forbid them not: for of such is the kingdom of God" (Mark 10:14).

Are little children supposed to suffer? she whispered to herself. She didn't know the answer. As she lay there, a song from Greystone came to mind:

Jesus loves me, this I know,
For the Bible tells me so;
Little ones to him belong;
They are weak, but he is strong.

But no one wanted her. Everyone always left her. How could this Jesus love her?

8

"What're you doin' mopin' around like this?" Nurse Halloran pushed the curtains aside and stepped in. She was
not in her uniform but instead wore a bright blue suit.
Her hat was covered with feathers and bows, and she was
carrying a large package wrapped in brown paper.

"Have I got news for you, Miss Austin." She plunked
the package down on the bed. "You're going on a trip. On
a train. Have you ever been on a train before?"

Ivy shook her head.

"Well, day after tomorrow, you'll be riding on one." The
nurse smiled broadly. "So what do you think of that?"

"I-I don't know," Ivy stammered.

"You'll be traveling with some other children to a town
in Arkansas. Some very nice people are waiting to take
you into their home and make you part of their family!"

"But what about the circus?"

"Good-bye and good riddance, I say." The nurse's
mouth was set in a firm line.

Ivy sat upright. "You mean they're not coming for me?
I'm not going back?"

"I should say not!" Nurse Halloran announced with a
jerk of her chin. "Now, don't you want to see what I've

brought you?" Without waiting for an answer, she began to untie the strings of the package.

The next morning, Ivy held Nurse Halloran's hand as they trudged down the hospital corridor for the last time. Ivy was wearing the gray and green plaid suit the nurse had brought her. It was a little small across the shoulders and felt too tight under her arms. But Ivy didn't want to hurt the nurse's feelings, so she didn't say anything.

Some of the nurses at the desk waved to her before the elevator doors closed.

In the lobby, Nurse Halloran leaned down and gave Ivy a hug.

"I have to go back on duty now, Ivy. Mrs. Willoughby will be along soon." She put both her plump hands on either side of Ivy's face. "Don't worry. Everything's going to be fine."

Ivy noticed the nurse's blue eyes glistening.

"You're a real little trooper, Ivy."

With a rustle of her skirt and a squeak of her high-top shoes, Nurse Halloran turned and walked back through the elevator doors. She didn't look back.

•

The winter morning air felt cold and smelled like coal soot as Ivy and Mrs. Willoughby rode in the cab to the train station. When the cab swerved to a jolting halt among a throng of other carriages, Ivy spotted a sign in metal letters that spelled out UNION RAILROAD STATION. The woman fumbled in her black purse then thrust some bills at the driver as they got down.

"Here, you carry this." Mrs. Willoughby handed Ivy the small bag Nurse Halloran had packed for her.

The huge depot echoed with their footsteps as they crossed the marble floor. They quickly rushed through another set of doors out onto the cement platform overlooking rows of twisting railroad tracks. At the other end, Ivy could see a group of children huddled around two women and a man.

"What kept you?" one of the ladies asked Mrs. Willoughby.

"I had to stop at St. Luke's to pick up this girl," she answered. "A last minute addition. Can you add her to your list?"

With an annoyed look, the other woman brought out a leather-backed clipboard and opened a fountain pen. "What's the name?"

"Ivy Austin. She's one of the children for Brookdale, Arkansas."

Just then the loud shriek of a train whistle pierced the air. Ivy shuddered so hard she wanted to run and huddle under a blanket. The sound always made her feel so alone. She was certainly alone now.

"All right, line up children," the man directed. "Move smartly now."

As Ivy moved into the row with the others, she felt a tug on her sleeve. When she turned her head, a little girl with a round face and golden blond bangs looked at her. Her eyes were brimming with tears.

"What's the matter?" Ivy whispered.

"I'm scared," she lisped.

"Don't worry. It'll be fun. You'll see." Ivy moved forward with the others. "What's your name?"

"Allison," was the soft reply.

"Mine's Ivy. We'll be friends."

As she boarded the train that day, Ivy decided to make a brand-new start. She wouldn't think about Paulo anymore and how the circus people had left her. She wouldn't waste any time grieving over Gyppo, Sophia, or Liselle, who hadn't even said good-bye. She was going to go on with her life.

The long days on the train trip were kept lively by the antics of some of the boy orphans, especially a freckle-faced one named Bunty Dugan. He was a cutup, teasing the girls and playing tricks and generally getting into mischief. His antics tried the patience of Mrs. Willoughby, who finally threw up her hands, declaring, "Land sakes, boy! What am I going to do with you?" It was, however, all in good fun, and Bunty became good friends with Ivy, who had earned his respect with her stories about life in the circus.

Throughout the trip, Allison stuck to Ivy like a postage stamp. Even though they had completely different personalities, Allison quiet and shy, Ivy outgoing and vivacious, they were soon inseparable, sharing everything. Ivy found the trip filled with interesting things to see out the windows. Of course, she was used to traveling, while this was Allison's first time ever away from the shelter of the orphanage, where she had lived since she was a baby. She had never seen the high mountains, the wide rivers, the rolling plains over which the train rumbled to its destination, Brookdale, Arkansas.

"We'll be arriving in Brookdale today, children," Mrs. Willoughby announced on the morning of the fifth day. "It's November 18, and this is our stop."

A stir of excitement rippled through the car. Ivy felt a twinge of fear. Her heart pounded at the thought of being paraded like a bunch of circus animals. She remembered how the elephants had been poked and prodded into line for the entrance march. Her stomach turned over slowly.

Ivy looked at Allison. She had the face of an angel with long, golden curls and a dimple at the corner of her mouth. On the other hand, Ivy's dark hair was still short, and her olive-colored skin made her look foreign. Her permanent teeth were in only part of the way, so her smile was still uneven. What could she do to make sure she was one of the first ones picked?

Ivy squirmed in the wool jacket Nurse Halloran had given her. It was too tight. She hated these clothes. Again she looked at Allison. No matter what *she* had on, Allison would be chosen first thing.

Then Ivy's eyes looked more closely. Allison was wearing a loose-fitting brightly flowered dress with a round collar and long puffed sleeves. It was really too big for her. And Ivy's clothes were too tight. All she had to do was to convince Allison that they needed to trade outfits!

A short while later, the sound of wheels braking on the steel rails reached their ears.

"Brookdale! Brookdale!" the conductor announced.

Mrs. Willoughby quickly inspected the hands and faces of the children. The trip had been a long one, and she had a headache today. She would be glad when this whole trip was over. There were so many children, and she had such a hard time keeping them straight. Thank goodness, this was their stop.

The woman straightened collars, tucked in shirttails, and brushed unruly hair. When the train jerked to a stop, she hustled them off and onto the platform.

No sooner had she lined them up inside the station than a lady walked up to her. "Mayor and Mrs. Ellison have just arrived. Which is the little girl who's to go with them?"

Mrs. Willoughby's mind went blank for a moment. Ellison? Now where had she seen that name? Oh yes. That was the name tape she had just seen on the hem of the little gypsy-looking girl's flowered dress. She was glad she'd taken the time to sew the right name tag on the clothes of the children being adopted.

"Allison," Mrs. Willoughby said aloud. The name, Ellison, had been spelled with an "A" on the name tape, but no matter. Mrs. Willoughby grabbed Ivy by the hand. "Here, child. There's your new family."

A handsome well-dressed couple had just entered the station's waiting room. The lady wore a violet bonnet with ribbons that almost matched her beautiful eyes. Her face was smooth with round, peach-bloom cheeks. She was the most beautiful person Ivy had ever seen.

Ivy felt a push. "Go on," Mrs. Willoughby's voice sounded irritated. "Those are the Ellisons. They're waiting over there."

Then Ivy saw another woman moving toward them. This one walked with an awkward gait. One of her legs was shorter than the other. A cripple! Instinctively, she drew back, holding her breath.

Should she tell Mrs. Willoughby that she and Allison had traded dresses? Would they be punished? One thing she had learned at Greystone and the circus—never say too much. It took only a fraction of a second for her to decide.

The lovely lady held out both hands as Ivy stepped forward.

9

"Come on, darling." Ivy felt Mrs. Ellison squeeze her hand as she went with her new mother out the door. A splendid dark green carriage hitched to a handsome black horse waited at the curb.

"In you go, little one." Mr. Ellison lifted Ivy inside.

"Are you cold?" Mrs. Ellison drew her close. "Such a thin little dress. But don't worry, you can put on some of the pretty things I bought you when we get home."

Ivy managed a smile but felt a mounting excitement mixed with fear. What would happen if they found out they had the wrong child? What if Mrs. Willoughby realized she had sent Ivy with the wrong people?

This all seemed too good to be true. Mrs. Ellison was so beautiful with her satiny white skin and wide eyes. She smelled like crushed violets.

After a short drive, Mr. Ellison boomed, "Here we are! Home!"

Ivy looked out the carriage window as they pulled up in front of a two-story yellow frame house. Dark green shutters framed the windows. Flowers bordered the walk leading up to a wide porch.

This was the kind of home Ivy had always imagined! Did dreams really come true? If this was a dream, she didn't want to wake up. Not ever.

Ivy followed Mrs. Ellison upstairs. Her eyes opened wide as she gazed at the white iron bed with its pink spread. Candy-striped curtains covered the windows, and a pink dresser sat in a corner near a ruffle-skirted dressing table.

Mrs. Ellison picked up the hairbrush and began stroking Ivy's hair. "It's so beautiful, Ivy, but we must let it grow, don't you think? Then we can put ribbons in it."

Ivy was thrilled. Her boyish look would be gone forever!

"Would you like to see what else I have for you?" Mrs. Ellison went over and opened the closet. Hanging there were several dresses, and on the shelf below, a row of new shoes.

"For me?"

"Of course, for you, sweetheart! You're going to be our little girl now. Let's put one of these on, shall we?"

She selected a scarlet dress with a wide sailor collar trimmed with dark blue braid. "Do you like this one?"

Ivy nodded.

"Here, raise your arms."

Mrs. Ellison pulled off the flowered dress Ivy had traded with Allison. Ivy watched her bundle up the dress with its name tape and toss it into the wastebasket. She felt an enormous sense of relief. The dress was gone. Now no one would know she had been placed out to the wrong people.

In spite of this, Ivy lived the next few days in dread. Day after day, she expected the doorbell to ring and Mrs.

Willoughby to be standing there, demanding that Ivy leave at once. But a week passed, then another, and still another, and nothing happened.

Every night after Mrs. Ellison tucked her in between the lavender-scented sheets, Ivy thought about her friend Allison. She prayed very hard that her friend's new home was as warm and loving as the Ellison home was. When she started school soon, she would find out.

On the first day of fourth grade, Ivy eagerly looked for her friend on the playground. As soon as the recess bell rang, she saw Allison coming from the third-grade classroom. Instantly, her worries about her new friend were put to rest.

Allison looked like a newly dressed doll from a toy shop. Her golden hair hung in long curls tied with crisp blue ribbons, and her blue dress had a lace-edged collar and cuffs. She carried a shiny red lunch pail.

"Oh, Ivy, I'm so glad to see you!" Allison burst out.

"Let's go eat at the bench down there so we can talk," Ivy suggested.

As they pulled out their sandwiches, Ivy learned that Allison had been adopted by Miss Fay, the woman with the crippled leg.

"What's it like?" Ivy asked, dreading what Allison might say.

Her friend took a bite of her ham and cheese sandwich. "It's very nice."

"Does she want you to call her Mama?" Mrs. Ellison had asked Ivy to call her Mother, and Ivy had agreed.

Allison shook her head. "No. Since she's not married, she says it wouldn't be proper. So I'm to call her Aunty."

"What's her house like?" Ivy was curious.

"It's small and white and has a garden in back with flowers and two birdhouses. Aunty loves animals. Miss Muffet is her cat. She stays inside and sits on the kitchen windowsill. Aunty says she scares the birds away if she goes outside."

"Do you have a room of your own?"

Allison took another bite and nodded. "It has flowered wallpaper and little windows that look out over the garden. Aunty sleeps in the next room. We leave our doors open at night so we can call back and forth if we want to.

"She has a sewing room in the front of the house too, because she makes clothes for people. She made this for me. Do you like it?" Allison smoothed her skirt.

"Yes, it's very pretty." Ivy rushed on. "So, do you think you'll like living with her?" She was still a bit worried.

"Oh yes!" Allison exclaimed. "Aunty is ever so nice, the nicest person I've ever met."

Ivy hesitated a moment. "And you don't mind that she's a . . . I mean, that she walks, well, funny?"

Allison's curls bounced as she shook her head. "Oh no! She told me all about how it happened. When she was a little girl, she fell out of a wagon. The wheel ran over her leg and crushed the bone. It never grew like her other leg did. That's why she limps."

Ivy's own accident came back to her, filling her with horror. What if she had been crippled? Would anyone have wanted to adopt her?

The bell rang and recess was over. The two friends gathered up the remains of their lunches and stuffed them back into their pails.

"Do you think I could come over and see you one day after school?" Ivy asked as they walked back toward their classrooms.

"Oh yes! Aunty says she wants me to have my friends over. I told her all about you and the others on the train." Allison smiled.

"I wonder how Bunty is doing. I saw him leave with a big, red-faced man who was pulling him along by the arm. Bunty didn't look too happy."

"Oh, Bunty, he'll do fine. He's tough," Ivy said confidently.

"See you later," Allison called as they hurried back to class.

Even though Ivy gradually met others, Allison still remained her special friend. Assured Allison was happy with Miss Fay, Ivy was free of her guilt. In spite of switching dresses with Allison, things had worked out for both of them. Ivy soon settled into life with the Ellisons. Then something happened that shook her feelings of security.

One winter evening on returning from the frozen pond in the park where she had been ice-skating with friends, Ivy opened the door to the toolshed, where she kept her skates. She heard a hoarse voice whisper her name. "Ivy!" She started to scream, but a rough hand clapped itself over her mouth.

"Don't scream, Ivy. It's me, Bunty. Bunty Dugan."

The wild pounding in her heart subsided. With mittened fingers, Ivy pried the hand away then twisted around so she could make out the figure in the darkness. In the dim light slanting in from the one high window, she saw the boy's familiar but frightened face. "Bunty! What are you doing here?"

"I've run away. Couldn't take it no more, Ivy. That man, Tolgrav, was too mean—mean clear through. We never got enough to eat. Never. And no milk, even though he has four cows. Worked us from sunup till dark. He was supposed to send us to school, but he didn't . . ." The words choked off and Bunty's voice hardened. "He didn't do nothin' for us he promised."

"But where are you going? What will you do?"

"I'm gonna hop a freight train. I been listenin' and there's a train just before eleven at night. I just come here to wait. He won't miss me till mornin' when I'm 'spected to do my chores. I wondered if you . . ." He paused, then stumbled on. "I'm real hungry, Ivy. Do you think you could get me some grub? Maybe somethin' to take with me?"

All the memories Ivy had pushed away suddenly rushed back. She recalled Bunty's cheerful grin, how he had bolstered their spirits on the Orphan Train, amusing them with his jokes. He had joshed with Allison so she wouldn't be afraid and had assured Ivy that things were going to be better when they got to Arkansas.

Well, he'd been right about *her*. But evidently things hadn't been better for Bunty. She owed him. But how could she manage to pack food and sneak it out to the toolshed?

While she hesitated, Bunty said, "I hate to ask, Ivy. I don't want to get you in no trouble. Maybe I better push on . . . I just couldn't think of nowhere else to go."

Quickly, Ivy gathered her wits. "No, of course not, Bunty. I just had to take a minute to think. It'll be all right. It might be a little while before I can get back out here, but don't worry. I'll come."

Ivy knew she had to help Bunty. She could get him enough food from the bountiful supplies in the Ellisons' kitchen and pantry, but she would have to be careful not to get caught. The Mayor and Mrs. Ellison were going out that evening, so Ivy ate supper in the kitchen with Bertha. She then sweetly offered to do the dishes so the cook could sit in her chair by the stove and read the paper. Soon the sound of gentle snoring told Ivy that Bertha had dozed off. Quickly, Ivy gathered bread, cheese, a few slices of roast beef, some apples, and a large piece of gingerbread and put them in a basket and slipped out of the house.

Outside in the freezing air, she ran to the shed where a shivering Bunty still hid. Ivy thrust the basket into his cold hands.

"I can't stay, Bunty. Here's some money. It's not much, but my allowance isn't due and I spent most of last month's."

"Thanks, Ivy. It's more'n I 'spected."

Ivy's eyes filled with tears. "Good luck, Bunty!" she whispered, her throat choked and hurting. Then she turned and ran back through the yard and into the house.

Later, when she went to bed, she could hear rain on the roof. She tried not to cry as she heard the steady downpour get louder and louder. She bit her lip, reminded of other long-ago nights when she had lain in the dark and listened to the drumbeat of the rain.

She thought of Bunty, crawling out of the toolshed and making his way down to the railroad tracks to wait until the train slowed at the crossing. She imagined him running and jumping, hoping to catch the handle on one of the boxcars and swing himself up to safety.

Ivy started to shiver and could not stop. She was terrified, thinking of Bunty out in the dark and the cold rain, running for his life. It had just been luck, "dumb luck," as Gyppo used to say, that it was Bunty not Ivy who had been placed out at the Tolgrav farm.

Then in the distance the mournful sound of a train whistle echoed through the night. Ivy shuddered, squeezed her eyes tight, and felt salty tears roll down her cheek as she burrowed into the pillows.

10

The Ellisons knew nothing about Ivy's life before Brookdale, and they didn't seem to care. Mercedes Ellison loved Ivy a great deal. She and her husband had never been able to have children, so Ivy was very special to them. Dan Ellison had fallen in love with the little girl the moment he had set eyes on her. He took pride in introducing her as "his daughter" and in taking her with him on his political rounds as well as on weekend fishing trips.

As the months passed, Ivy's life was so full and rich that she began to feel secure. Ivy was aware of her good fortune, and she did everything to please her adoptive parents. She felt real affection for Mother and Daddy Dan.

It was a busy household. Mayor and Mrs. Ellison did a great deal of entertaining. They also went out two or three evenings a week to events and civic functions. On such evenings, Ivy loved to go into Mercedes's dressing room and watch her get ready.

Of all the rooms in the house, Ivy liked this room best. The furniture was pale gray wood painted with roses. A dressing table with a full-length mirror sat in an alcove surrounded by three windows. While she brushed her hair, Mercedes would let Ivy try on her hats or sample perfume. Ivy loved every minute of it.

Summer came, then another fall and the school year of 1889. Allison, who was bright, skipped a grade and was promoted, so the two girls were in the fifth grade together.

Ivy often visited the little house on Maple Lane where Allison lived. It reminded her of the cottages she used to see with Gyppo when they'd tack up circus posters. Ivy enjoyed her visits. She and Allison would go into the kitchen where Aunty Fay would serve them cookies and cocoa. While she sewed, Fay would ask them questions about their day. Often a fire would be glowing through the shiny black stove, casting a bright reflection on the copper pots hanging on the walls. Rows of blue and white china filled a tall polished oak hutch. Pots of red geraniums lined the windowsill where Miss Muffet basked in the sun.

One day, the girls were nibbling chocolate chip cookies in the garden.

"Do you ever think of the Orphan Train, Ivy?" Allison asked.

Startled, Ivy looked at her. "Sometimes, I guess. Why?"

"I do. I think of before that too . . . when I was in the orphanage. I didn't know my parents."

"Thinking about it'll just make you sad. You're happy now with Aunty Fay, aren't you?"

Allison set her glass of lemonade on the little round table. "Oh yes. Aunty is the sweetest person in the world, and I love her dearly. But I suppose it's only natural to wonder what your life would've been like if your real mother hadn't given you up."

"She probably had to, Allison," Ivy offered. "For lots of reasons. Maybe she was too sick or poor to take care of you."

"I know, it's just that . . ." and Allison's voice trailed off.

"Let's go play with Miss Muffet's kittens." Ivy grabbed Allison's hand and pulled her along.

The subject was never discussed again, but it disturbed Ivy. Allison's comment had stirred something deep within her, something she didn't want to feel. Even though both of them seemed happy on the surface, there were still scars deep down inside.

One evening in May, the Ellisons sat together at the dinner table.

"I've bought a whole block of tickets to a circus," Mr. Ellison announced as he buttered a slice of warm bread. "It's scheduled to come to Brookdale this Saturday." He turned to Ivy. "Why don't you invite your class, Ivy?"

Like a puppet whose strings are jerked, Ivy felt a jolt. She dropped her soup spoon with a clatter.

"What's the matter, darling?" Mercedes asked with alarm.

"She's excited, that's all." The mayor beamed.

"No, it's something else, Dan," his wife replied. "What is it, Ivy?"

"I feel sick," Ivy said weakly, pressing her hands tightly over her stomach.

She really did. But it wasn't just her stomach. Her mind felt sick too. What if this was the Higgins Brothers' Circus? What if she saw Paulo? Worse still, what if he saw *her* and demanded she come back to the Tarantinos' act? After all, he had the papers from Greystone.

Ivy ran a temperature for the next several days. When she returned to school the following week, her friends told her she had missed the circus. All Ivy felt was relief.

11

One day at the end of seventh grade, Ivy met Allison in the cloakroom after the dismissal bell.

"Congratulations, Allison. I'm so glad you won the art prize for your poster."

Allison beamed. She had worked hard for the Arbor Day contest.

"And I've got my patch for being on the girls' winning tennis team. So come on. All of us are going to Phelan's Soda Shop to celebrate the end of school." Ivy pulled a dollar bill out of her pocket. "My treat!"

Allison put her sketch pad and paint box into her book bag. "What do you mean *all of us?*"

"Well, my tennis team of course, and Sue Finch and Mary Anne Bryson and—I don't know who all—most of the class."

"Even Ginny Colby?" Allison raised her eyebrows.

"I guess so. If she wants to."

Allison buckled the straps on her book bag carefully then looked directly at Ivy. "Why do you always feel you have to buy friends, Ivy?"

Tears sprang into Ivy's eyes. "That's the meanest thing anyone has ever said to me!" she gasped. "And I thought you were my friend!" With that, Ivy whirled around and ran out into the corridor.

Daddy Dan was always giving her money and telling her to take her friends to the sweet shop for an ice-cream cone. So why shouldn't she? Yet, Allison's question bothered her all through the night. Did her friends like her for herself or what she did for them?

The next day Ivy ignored Allison on the playground, and when the bell rang for classes to begin, she walked right past her without a glance. During geography, Allison passed Ivy a note.

"I'm sorry. Please meet me at recess," it read.

At recess, Allison waited outside the classroom door. "Let's go to the far end, our old place, where we ate lunch together when we first came to Brookdale," she suggested.

Reluctantly, Ivy agreed.

"Oh, Ivy, I'm so sorry about yesterday," Allison began. "I don't know why I said such a hateful thing. It just burst out. I think I was hoping just you and I could go somewhere after school. I don't know, it's just that everything seems so easy for you."

"Easy?" Ivy was amazed. "It's you who has it easy, Allison! You're so talented. Everybody thinks you're such a good artist." Ivy halted.

"Ivy, you're my very best friend. I didn't mean to hurt you. Do you forgive me?"

"Sure, Allison, I do," she replied as she bit into her apple tart.

That was the end of the incident between the two friends, but its impact lingered with Ivy for years to come. What people thought of her was important. She had to admit that. But she also had to admit how precious her friendship was with Allison.

That summer Fay married a talented cabinetmaker from Brookdale named Matthew Lund. While the couple was on their honeymoon, Allison stayed with the Ellisons.

"Are they really in love, Allison?" Ivy asked one day.

"They got married, didn't they, silly?"

"But do they kiss and hug and all that?"

"Not in front of me."

"But Aunty Fay—" Ivy hesitated. "She's as nice as can be, but she isn't very pretty, Allison, and well, how can someone like her, being lame and all."

Allison's face got beet red. "She can do anything any other wife can do and lots better too! She can sew and cook and garden and everything."

"You needn't get all huffy about it," Ivy replied. "I just wondered, that's all."

Ivy had to take Allison's word that it was true. But this marriage was giving her many things to think about. Perhaps it was what people were like on the inside that mattered. She remembered the time Sophia had pointed to her heart and told her not to let anyone change the inside. Maybe it wasn't necessary to be handsome or beautiful to find lasting love and happiness.

"Well, you don't need to wonder anymore. He's in love with her and that's that!"

Ivy quickly changed the subject. "Say, let's do something fun." She twirled around and then stopped. "I know! Let's go down to the river. It's warm enough to wade. We can take off our shoes and stockings."

Allison seemed to hesitate.

"Oh, come on. We'll stop at Fallons' and get some candy bars and sarsaparilla. We'll have a picnic too." Ivy grabbed her friend's hand.

Fallons' was a general store, carrying all kinds of merchandise from men's overalls to tools to candies and crackers. The bell jangled as the two girls entered. Mr. Fallon was stocking the shelves. Mrs. Fallon sat behind the cash register and glanced at them over her spectacles.

The girls browsed around until Ivy spotted two wide-brimmed straw hats in a corner. "Oh, look, Allison. These would be perfect to wear to the river." She picked them up, jammed one on Allison's head, and placed the other at an angle on her own.

"If you try on them hats, you have to buy 'em." Mrs. Fallon's voice was sharp.

Immediately, Allison took off the hat and looked at the price tag dangling from the brim. "The hats are thirty-nine cents, Ivy. I don't have enough money."

Something in Mrs. Fallon's voice had made Ivy mad. "Never mind. It'll be all right," she whispered.

Ivy caught Allison's hand and dragged her toward the candy display, still wearing the straw hat.

"Didn't you hear me?" Mrs. Fallon leaned forward. "I said you'd have to pay for the hats if you tried 'em on."

"We're taking them." Ivy smiled sweetly.

Ivy then darted around the store, picking up other items. When she had finished, she piled them on the counter—rock candy, two palmetto fans, a box of cookies, some hair ribbons, and a package of mints.

Mrs. Fallon pressed her lips together, her eyes squinting. "That comes to two dollars and ninety-three cents."

Ivy lifted her chin and replied, "Charge it to my parents' account. That's *Mayor* and Mrs. Ellison." With that, she swooped up the bag and marched toward the door with Allison hurrying along after her.

"That's that orphan child, Wilbur, the one the mayor adopted," Ivy heard Mrs. Fallon say as she started out the door. It struck her like an arrow. Anger, swift and hot, swept over her. She tossed her head. "Come on, Allison, let's go."

The two girls ran down the steps and didn't stop running until they had gotten to the grassy banks of the river at the far end of town.

"What an old witch!" Ivy exclaimed as she flung herself down, panting. "I'll never step foot in that store again as long as I live!"

12

Ivy was late. It was her first morning at Brookdale High. She had fussed so long with her curly hair that she didn't even have time for breakfast. Hurrying down the hall to the gym for the first assembly, she collided with a tall young man with a shock of sandy hair.

"Oh, I'm so sorry," she exclaimed, out of breath.

The nice-looking young man swung open the door for her, and they both slipped inside. Ivy found the nearest seat at the back, while he strode right up to the front and took a seat on the stage. After Mr. Stanton, the principal, made the welcoming speech, he introduced the teachers. Then he asked the people on stage to stand.

"Of course, this young man needs no introduction." Mr. Stanton chuckled. "Everyone here knows Baxter McNeil, our student body president and editor of our school newspaper." A round of applause rippled through the crowd.

The school newspaper, the Brookdale High *Banner,* was published twice a month. Hoping to get to know the handsome editor, Ivy decided to try out for the job of class reporter. However, as the school year moved into full swing, she was caught up in many events, enjoying them rather than reporting on them.

"Ivy, I'm going to the *Banner* office." Allison had done a pen and ink sketch of the class emblem and motto. "The deadline is Friday. Want me to take your report?"

"I haven't written it yet," Ivy replied with a wave of her hand as the two of them attended the first freshman class meeting. "There's not much to report."

"We've had class elections. You could give the names of the officers. We've also voted to have a booth at the fall carnival."

"I can do it tonight and turn it in tomorrow." Ivy picked up her books and sweater.

"I've got to get to my art lesson with Mr. Bristow," Allison said. "See you later."

That evening, instead of writing her report, Ivy spent her time washing her hair. She totally forgot about the deadline until she spotted Allison the next day.

"Why'd you volunteer for the job of class reporter if you didn't want to do it?" Allison asked.

Ivy spoke softly so the students walking by them would not hear. "Because I thought it'd be a good way to meet Baxter McNeil."

"Well, you'd better get something in!"

Ivy spent recess huddled over a notepad, scribbling a hasty report. Then she hurried down the hallway to the newspaper office. Baxter sat at a cluttered desk.

"Hello. I'm Ivy Ellison," she said in her sweetest voice. "I'm the freshman class reporter, and I'm here to turn in my copy."

"You're late," he replied with a steady gaze. "You've nearly missed the deadline. Copy's supposed to be put in the box over there before lunch on Friday. I was just getting ready to leave for the printer's." He held out his hand. "Let me see it. If there are too many corrections, your piece may not make this issue."

Ivy handed it to him and stood there. After scanning the page, he flung it down. "That's the sloppiest piece of copy anyone has ever turned in. Most freshmen try to do their best. I can't even read this."

"But . . . but the names are all right there . . ."

"Look, Miss Iverson—or whatever your name is—if you can't do better than this—"

"But I can! I mean, I *will*. Please give me another chance," she pleaded. "I could write it over, right now."

Baxter hesitated. He probably should teach this girl a lesson about deadlines. But her dark eyes were so wide and anxious. "Well, all right. But don't let it happen again."

That meeting set the tone for Ivy's relationship with Baxter for the rest of the year. But Ivy still had a crush on him and tried hard to be a better reporter. Her writing did improve, but the senior editor never really seemed to notice her.

"Someday Baxter McNeil's going to beg me to go out with him," she declared as she and Allison were studying for final exams.

"Oh, Ivy. It's been a whole year, and he hasn't made the slightest move."

"Well, someday he will."

The years in high school passed quickly. At long last, Ivy and Allison were seniors. Soon they would be graduating.

A soft June breeze billowed the curtains of the window in Ivy's bedroom. It was the last week of school. She and

Allison were working on their scrapbooks, the ones they had been keeping since their first week of high school.

"I know you'll get the art award," Ivy told Allison as she pasted in a clipping about her last tennis tournament of the year. "Your posters were always the best."

Allison didn't comment. She simply put the finishing touches on a flower border she was painting around the page that would eventually hold her diploma.

The two friends worked in silence for a few minutes. Then Ivy asked, "Do you think you can go with Mother and me to Acacia Springs this summer, Allison?"

Ivy looked over at her.

"It was Mother's idea. She thinks you're a good influence on me." Ivy laughed.

"I'd love to, Ivy, but I can't." Allison set her glue down on the floor. "You know I'm hoping for that scholarship at the art school in St. Louis. Mr. Bristow put together a portfolio of my paintings and sent them with his recommendation."

Ivy was thrilled for her friend. "That's wonderful, Allison. But you could still come. School doesn't start until September. We could have the whole summer together. No lessons, no books. Just fun."

Allison picked up the scissors to snip around the edges of an invitation to the senior class breakfast. "I have to get a job to help with the expenses, Ivy. Even with the scholarship, it'll cost a lot of money. You know, train fare, room and board, art supplies. I can't expect Aunty to do it all."

Ivy was silent. The old shadow of guilt descended, twisting her stomach with its grip. If she had spoken up that day so long ago with Mrs. Willoughby, it would have been *Allison* not *Ivy* who went to the Ellisons. If they had adopted Allison, she wouldn't need to work all summer or even get a scholarship. The mayor could have sent her to the best art school in the country.

A few days later, Ivy decided to take a walk down to the river. The memories of what she had done so long ago were haunting her again. Even if she confessed at this late date, the mess couldn't be straightened out. Ivy plopped down on the grass beside the water. How could she ever explain? How would she ever be forgiven?

She buried her face in her hands, trying to think things through. She hadn't wanted to hurt Allison, and Allison *did* seem happy enough now. If everyone found out, though, Ivy would be branded a liar. She'd be hated and have to leave town. From deep within her, a well of tears broke through. She heard her own wrenching sobs.

"Ivy?"

She thought she heard her name.

"Ivy? What on earth's the matter? Are you hurt?"

Pushing her hair back from her wet forehead, Ivy looked up into the face of Baxter McNeil. Of all people! She had not seen him since he had graduated three years before and gone off to the state university. Ivy hastily wiped her eyes with the back of her hands.

"Baxter McNeil! You're the last person I expected to see." Ivy struggled to sit up and smooth her wrinkled skirt. "What're you doing here?"

"Fishing," he answered dryly. He crouched down beside her and set his fishing pole on the ground. "Can I do something to help?"

"Oh no. I played hooky and came running down here and twisted my ankle. It hurts." Ivy wasn't about to tell him the truth. "So, how's college?"

"It's fine. I've got a summer job on a newspaper in St. Louis near the university. It starts on the twentieth." Baxter gazed downriver toward the glistening sun. "I didn't realize how much I'd miss this place. Good old Brookdale. Couldn't wait to get away. Now I can't wait to get back."

"You mean you want to come back?"

Baxter looked around and nodded. "I miss the small town where everyone knows you. I've already talked to Mr. Barnes, the editor of the *Brookdale Messenger*, about a job as a reporter when I graduate."

Baxter picked up his fishing pole, unwound his long frame, and got to his feet. Then he reached down for her hand to pull her up. "Do you think you can manage to walk back to town on your ankle now?"

Ivy had almost forgotten her fib. "It's all right, I think."

The couple walked slowly back up the road toward town. At the Ellisons' gate, she paused. "Well, good-bye, Baxter. It was nice seeing you again."

"You too, Ivy." His eyes regarded her steadily for a moment. "Have a nice summer." With a wave, he turned and walked down the street.

Baxter was better looking than ever. As Ivy watched him go, she felt a pang of disappointment. Hmph! She remembered her mad crush on him. But she had gotten over that, hadn't she?

13

The gymnasium of Brookdale High School had been transformed into a palace ballroom. The entrance was flanked by posts wrapped in paper that looked like marble. Flickering candles in papier-mâché lamps cast rainbow-colored lights on the floor, now waxed and polished for dancing. A banner proclaiming "Class of 1897" adorned the door. When the seniors entered, they walked into an enchanted fairyland.

"How'd you ever manage it?" Ivy clutched Allison's arm in excitement.

"We decorated it like a picture I found in *Arabian Nights,*" her friend replied. "Does it work?"

"Does it ever! You're an artistic genius!"

As the decorating chairman, Allison enjoyed everyone's excitement. When the class president whisked her off to dance, Ivy was left alone.

"May I have this dance?" The deep voice was behind her.

Ivy spun around. "Baxter! What're you doing here?"

"The alumni were issued invitations. We're having our class reunion later this week. Shall we?" He held out his arm to escort her onto the dance floor.

Surprised, Ivy picked up her skirt and floated into his arms as the orchestra began playing.

"You're looking lovely tonight, Ivy."

"You look splendid yourself, Baxter." She smiled.

"I was afraid your dance card would be filled," he began as they shuffled across the floor.

"To tell you the truth, four years ago, I would've killed for a chance to dance with you."

He seemed shocked. "You should've told me. I would've invited you to my graduation dance."

"No, you wouldn't have. Remember? I was—in your words—the worst excuse for a class reporter you'd ever seen!"

"Good grief, Ivy, are you quoting me directly? I couldn't have been that rude, could I?"

Her eyes sparkled and the music continued.

"Would you accept my apology?" He looked at her longingly. "I guess there are a lot of things about you I need to know."

"Like what?" she asked as they danced to the band's rhythm.

"Everything."

"Everything? No, that's not a good idea." Ivy shook her head. "There should be some mystery somewhere."

"You're probably right." His hand holding hers tightened. "Especially someone you care about."

Suddenly, Ivy found it hard to breathe. She and Baxter circled the room again.

"How much longer are you going to be in Brookdale, Baxter?"

"Two weeks."

"Well, that should give us enough time, shouldn't it?" she asked softly.

The following two weeks were like a fairy tale come true. Baxter McNeil was actually taking her out! Ivy remembered the hours she had pined for him and how much she had wanted him to notice her. Now it was happening.

Two days before he was to leave, Baxter came for dinner at the Ellisons. Afterward, he and Ivy went for a walk in the summer dusk. When it began to get dark, they strolled slowly back to the house and sat down together on the side porch swing. A pale oval moon hung in the evening sky.

"You'll write me after I'm gone, won't you?" he asked.

"I'm not much good at letter writing, but I'll try."

He slipped his arm around her shoulder. For a few minutes the only sound was the swing's gentle squeak.

Then Ivy sighed. "I hate to have you go. The city seems a long way off."

"Not too far actually. And it's not as if it's forever. You know I plan to come back here and go to work at the *Messenger*."

"Are you sure you can get a job at the paper?"

"No, but I know I'll be back. Brookdale is my home. One day I want to be the editor of its newspaper."

The couple swung for a few minutes in silence, the swing creaking on its chains.

"I'm going to miss you, Baxter," Ivy said seriously.

"I'll be back," he replied.

Suddenly something deep within her moved. How many times in her life had she believed someone would come back? First her papa and then her mama. Then her three friends at the circus. Ivy understood what it was like to care deeply for people and never have them return. She knew what it meant to be abandoned. Could she dare to hope Baxter would return? Ivy didn't know. All she knew was that she never wanted to experience the feeling of abandonment again. Not ever.

Baxter leaned over and kissed her softly. "I know it's been fast, Ivy, but I love you."

That night, Ivy sat straight up in bed, not knowing what had awakened her. She waited, listening, then it came—the long, lonely sound of a train whistle echoing through the clear summer night.

The day after Baxter left, Ivy visited Allison. At her brief knock, Allison opened the door. "Oh, Ivy. I'm so glad you've come. I've just received the most wonderful news!"

Fay was right behind her. "Hello, Ivy. You're just in time to celebrate with us."

"What's happened?" She stepped inside.

"Here, read it yourself." Allison thrust a piece of stationery toward her.

It was a letter with the words "The Art Institute" across the top. Ivy scanned it. "Oh, Allison, how wonderful! I'm so proud of you!" Ivy hugged her.

Soon, Allison would be leaving for St. Louis. In spite of her genuine happiness over Allison's scholarship, Ivy felt strangely depressed when she got home that evening.

"I ran into Mr. Stapleton this afternoon, Ivy," Mercedes mentioned as they ate dinner. "He asked what your plans are, dear, and I told him we hoped you'd go to Elmhurst."

"I'm not interested in Elmhurst, Mother." Ivy's tone was firm.

Mercedes sipped her tea. "Have you looked at the brochures, darling? We could take a trip up there and visit."

Ivy placed her knife and fork on her plate. "I don't want to go away."

"But why not, Ivy?" Daddy Dan asked. "Elmhurst is one of the finest finishing schools in the state. We can easily afford to send you there. They offer so many advantages—piano and voice lessons. You could even learn horseback riding."

"I don't like horses!" Ivy's voice grew louder. "Not at all!" She quickly changed the subject. "Mother, I'm really not hungry anymore. I need to go shampoo my hair." Ivy quickly scooted her chair back and left the room.

No sooner had she gotten to her bedroom than she broke out in uncontrollable laughter. Horseback riding? If only her mother knew. Paulo and his tricks. The cracking of his whip. His awful rage. In seconds, however, her laughter had turned to tears. Ivy flung herself on her bed, buried her face in one pillow, and pulled another one over her head so no one could hear her sobs.

The summer passed by leisurely. Ivy and her mother visited Acacia Springs, a summer resort. When they returned in the fall, Allison had already left for St. Louis. Brookdale seemed impossibly empty to Ivy with both her best friend and Baxter gone.

Mercedes continued to try to interest Ivy in Elmhurst. At last, Ivy reluctantly agreed. It turned out to be an excellent decision. With its spacious grounds, winding paths, and brick buildings, Elmhurst provided the perfect place for Ivy to begin a whole new phase of her life. No one knew anything about her except that she was the daughter of Daniel Ellison, the mayor of Brookdale. Her letters home were happy ones, filled with news of her activities.

She did not, however, sign up for horseback riding.

When Ivy arrived home for Christmas, the Ellisons' house was gaily decorated, and a beautiful evergreen tree stood in the parlor waiting to be trimmed.

"Welcome home, darling!" Mercedes greeted her. "We're so glad you're here. We've missed you."

A handful of invitations to Christmas parties awaited Ivy. One she had to attend with her parents was the annual buffet at the home of the president of the Brookdale Savings and Loan. Dressed in a crimson velvet dress with her dark hair swirled high on her head, Ivy looked particularly charming.

"There's someone I want you to meet, dear," the hostess said shortly after they arrived. She took Ivy by the arm and led her toward a young man standing on the other side of the room. "Mr. Russell Trent, I'd like to present the mayor's daughter, Ivy Ellison."

Russell Trent was good-looking and well groomed. He was fashionably dressed in a dark suit with a high stiff collar and gray silk cravat.

"Delighted, Miss Ellison." He bowed over Ivy's extended hand. "I've heard a lot about you."

"I hope it was good," Ivy said flirtatiously.

The evening turned out to be quite entertaining. Russell and Ivy spent most of it together. Finally, her mother signaled it was time to leave. Ivy noticed that Russell did not seem to want her to go.

As he helped her on with her hooded velvet evening wrap, he asked, "May I call on you while you're home for the holidays?"

"By all means, Mr. Trent. I'd be very pleased." Secretly, she was flattered that she had so quickly sparked the interest of Brookdale's newest bachelor.

The very next day Russell sent Ivy a note, asking if he might call the following evening. He arrived with a bouquet of red roses and a box of chocolates. By the week's end, he appeared to be seriously courting her. The Ellisons were delighted. He was a personable young man, and his job at the Savings and Loan made his future look very bright.

One person who did not approve of the newcomer, however, was Allison. Home for the holidays, Allison kept her distance whenever they were at the same parties. Russell noticed this and mentioned it to Ivy one evening when he brought her home.

"Your friend doesn't like me."

"You must be mistaken," Ivy protested.

But the following afternoon, while Ivy and Allison wrapped Christmas presents together, Ivy told her what Russell had said.

"I think he's stuffy." She shrugged, tying a bright red ribbon around one package. "A bore. Full of himself. What do you see in him?"

"You must be blind!" Ivy replied. "He's just about the best-looking fellow in this town. And besides, he's charming and a splendid dancer."

"Is that all?"

"Isn't that enough?"

"Looks and manners don't mean anything, Ivy." Allison snipped the ends of the ribbon. "What do you talk about?"

"Talk? Well, we talk about . . . everything. Whatever comes to our minds."

"Have you forgotten about Baxter?"

"Baxter's different." Ivy shook her head. "He's so intelligent—"

"That's what I mean, Ivy. I've tried to carry on a conversation with your Mr. Trent. He has practically nothing important to say."

Russell had planned to spend Christmas in Cartersville with his family. The day before he was to leave, he stared out the window near his desk at the Savings and Loan. All morning long snow flurries had fallen on the sidewalk, now covered in white. The sky was an odd shade of gray blue, slung with low-hanging clouds.

Russell had been unable to apply himself to his work today. He couldn't seem to get Ivy Ellison out of his mind. When he wasn't with her, he thought about her constantly. She had taken hold of his waking thoughts as well as his dreams. Even though she wasn't really beautiful, there was something about her that attracted him. He enjoyed her zest for life. It balanced his own tendency to be moody. Ivy made him laugh.

Startled out of his thoughts, Russell heard a familiar voice. He swiveled his chair around just in time to see Ivy enter the bank. She looked stylishly smart in her red coat with its beaver collar and matching hat. She smiled and waved then went directly up to one of the teller's cages.

Russell left his desk and crossed the lobby to speak to her. "And what brings you out on this cold morning?" he asked.

"Money. Why else would anyone come to a bank?" she teased as she pulled off her gloves. "I have some Christmas shopping to do."

"You're pretty late, aren't you? It's nearly Christmas."

"I've added a few names to my list." A dimple appeared at one corner of her mouth.

A few minutes later, Ivy left. As she went out the door, the bank teller remarked, "That's a lovely young lady and a mighty lucky one too."

"Lucky?" Russell asked.

"Of course! She was one of the waifs brought here on the Orphan Train."

"Orphan Train?" Russell was puzzled.

"Never heard of it? Brought little kids from orphanages back East."

Russell slowly walked back to his desk. His mood had taken a decided turn for the worst. Ivy . . . an orphan? What would his mother say? After all, she had brought him up with background and breeding. Russell planned to go places and become someone. How would this fit in?

Distracted, he shuffled the loan applications on his desk. This was a new development. He had a lot to consider.

However, when Russell saw Ivy on the night of his return to Brookdale a week later, he put aside his misgivings. She looked so beautiful in her dress of midnight blue. After all, he thought, he didn't plan to remain in Brookdale all his life. He had higher ambitions. When he moved to a bigger bank somewhere else, who would even think to question his wife's background? Everything would be all right. She would still be known as the daughter of Brookdale's mayor. No, this girl could help him get ahead in life. She was the girl for him.

When the Valentine's Day dance became the main topic of conversation at Elmhurst, Ivy was forced to consider which young man to invite as her escort. Ever since meeting Russell, she had stopped writing letters to Baxter. She didn't know how to tell him she was caught up in a new romance.

Russell sent flowers and wrote little notes. Baxter was pinching pennies so he could complete his final year at school. Russell was self-assured and worldly. His position at the bank appealed to Ivy's yearning for acceptance and social status. Baxter didn't even have a job. It was true that Baxter was handsome, but the other girls sighed dreamily when they spotted Russell's picture on her dormitory room dresser.

Finally, Ivy decided to invite Russell, and for weeks after the holiday dance, she floated in a romantic mist. When florist boxes were delivered, the girls fluttered about while she read the enclosed cards. Ivy gloried in being the center of attention.

Yet, just under the surface, her deep dark secret lurked. Her life at Elmhurst and Russell's courtship helped her deny it was there. But she couldn't escape it forever. She was an orphan with no parents, someone who had once been a child performer in a circus. She had even lied to get where she was. Way down below, she feared that the truth would one day come to light.

One afternoon, Ivy and a friend were walking across campus to the sweet shop. As she passed a newsstand, she noticed the headline: CIRCUS STAR PLUNGES TO DEATH. Ivy halted.

"What's the matter?" her friend asked.

All Ivy could do was point to the paper. Her friend bought a copy and read the article. "The Higgins Brothers' star aerialist, Liselle Fortunato, was killed instantly yesterday when—"

The words spun out into the autumn air and hurled Ivy back to the smell of sawdust and the sound of the elephants. She saw herself standing in the doorway of Liselle's caravan, watching her put on her special ballet slippers. She could see her flying through the air in the big top.

"The performer was pronounced dead at the hospital," her friend continued reading.

Ivy felt dazed. Liselle, dead! No one at Elmhurst knew about her past, and no one *would* know. Ivy reminded herself that the circus had been a life she hated. They had all deserted her, left her forever, even Liselle.

"Come on, Ivy. Let's get our sodas." Her friend's voice broke through Ivy's sad thoughts.

Ivy stood up. "Yes, let's go."

But it was not easy for Ivy to forget. That night she lay sleepless in her bed. What had happened? How had Liselle fallen? Ivy thought about her first experience on the high wire. Had Liselle forgotten her own advice never to look down? Had she lost her concentration for a split second?

Now, Ivy wished she could have stayed in touch with the kind young woman who had befriended her so long ago. Now it was too late to tell Liselle how much she had meant to her.

"Oh, Liselle, I'm so sorry," Ivy moaned into her pillow. *"Adieu, ma cherie. Adieu."*

15

Ivy and her mother once again spent the summer at Acacia Springs. Russell came up two weekends in a row. The third weekend was magical. After dinner on Saturday night, the couple went to a dance at the pavilion. At one point, Russell waltzed her smoothly and gracefully out onto the porch.

"Let's take a walk down to the lake," he suggested.

Japanese lanterns strung between the leafy trees lined the walk. A pale round moon rose over the water, paving a path to the shore. Strains of music echoed through the soft summer air, a background to the rhythm of the water slapping the wooden pilings of the dock.

Humming under her breath, Ivy held her skirt and swayed to the melody. Russell caught her around the waist, and they danced slowly around and around.

"Ivy, I have something to ask you," he began. "Before I came, I went to see your father."

"Went to see Daddy? Whatever for?"

With one hand, he reached into the inside pocket of his blue flannel blazer and brought out a small box. "For this. It's . . . well, you'll see." He pressed the small spring, and the lid flew open. A perfect diamond ring glittered in the moonlight. "I want you to wear this. It's an engagement ring."

The Ellisons were very pleased with the match, and they welcomed Russell warmly. The September announcement in the *Brookdale Messenger* stated that a December wedding was being planned.

"But what about Baxter?" Allison demanded the next afternoon when she came to see Ivy.

"What about him?"

"How can you think of marrying Russell when you love Baxter?"

"I love Russ, Allison. He's everything I've ever wanted," Ivy retorted.

"I know you, Ivy Ellison. You can't tell me you don't love Baxter anymore."

"Of course, I love him." Ivy fingered her beautiful diamond ring. "But I love Russell more."

"Have you told Baxter?"

"No." Ivy frowned. "How could I? We just got home from the springs yesterday. You're the first one I've told. I thought you'd be happy for me."

Allison narrowed her eyes. "You know Baxter's coming home, Ivy. He got a job with the *Messenger* and will be home the end of the month. Didn't he write you?"

Ivy instantly thought about the two letters from Baxter now lying on her dressing table. She hadn't opened them yet.

"Maybe he planned to surprise you." Allison shook her head. "He's going to be heartbroken, Ivy. Please think about what you're doing." She sat down on the edge of the bed beside her friend. "You can't really be giving up a man like Baxter for someone like Russell, can you?"

Ivy bristled. "What do you mean 'someone like Russell'?"

"Anyone can see Russell is shallow. He isn't half the man Baxter is."

Ivy jumped up and flounced over to the window. "I thought you'd understand."

Allison got up to leave. "That's just it, Ivy. I do understand."

With that, she opened the door and left.

A few days later, Allison came over again. "I'm sorry if I hurt you, Ivy. I hope we'll always be friends."

Relieved, Ivy hugged her. "Of course, we will. And you'll be my maid of honor."

Although Allison still did not approve of the wedding, she agreed. She and Ivy had been friends too long to let this come between them.

"And I want Aunty Fay to make my gown. Will you design it for me?"

The two girls decided to go downtown to look at patterns. As they walked out of the one fabric store in town, they met Mrs. Fallon on the sidewalk. The owner of Fallons' Mercantile looked startled and then changed her expression into a tight smile.

"I read that you're engaged to be married, Miss Ellison," she said a little too sweetly. "We have expanded our merchandise in the past three years. Our stock now compares with any you might buy elsewhere." She directed her comments toward Ivy, completely ignoring Allison. "Please pass this on to your mother, won't you?"

Ivy remained calm in spite of her vivid memory of the shopkeeper's behavior so long ago. "Thank you, Mrs. Fallon. I'll certainly keep that in mind."

"The nerve of that woman!" Ivy exclaimed after she had left. "I wouldn't buy a spool of thread in her store!"

Two weeks later, Ivy was sitting in her window seat brushing her hair when the Ellisons' maid, Bertha, tapped at the door. "You have a caller, Miss Ivy."

"Who is it?"

"It's Mr. McNeil, miss."

Ivy's stomach plummeted. She should have written him and broken the news to him. Now she'd have to do it in person.

At the sound of her footsteps, Baxter spun around. He pulled a scrap of newsprint out of his pocket.

"So, you're engaged?" His voice was angry. "Funny, I should have to find out by reading it in my hometown newspaper. You didn't even have the decency to tell me yourself. Who is this fellow?"

"I just—" Ivy stammered. "Well, you know, we haven't been writing each other regularly, Baxter—"

"As I recall, I wrote. You didn't. The last time I heard from you was a postcard from Acacia Springs in June. You didn't mention anything about a Russell Trent."

"I don't owe you an explanation," Ivy defended herself loudly then softened. "I meant to write you, Baxter, honestly I did."

"Have you forgotten what we talked about last summer?"

"That was—"

"You're going to tell me that was then and this is now?" Baxter demanded. "Ivy, you knew I was going to come back here and try to get a job at the *Messenger*. I even turned down a job offer in St. Louis to come back here . . . because of you."

"I didn't know that, Baxter."

"I told you I loved you, Ivy. Doesn't that mean anything?"

"I'm sorry, Baxter."

"Sorry? Is that all, Ivy?"

"I didn't mean to hurt you. But while you were gone, I fell in love with Russ, and that's all I can say."

Ivy started to move away, but he grabbed her wrists. "I said I wouldn't believe it, not until I heard it from your lips. Tell me it isn't true, Ivy."

Ivy tried to free her wrists from Baxter's strong grip. "It *is* true, Baxter. I'm engaged. Russ and I are going to be married in December."

Baxter loosened his grasp. "Are you so needy for status and security that you'll do something you know isn't right? This fellow doesn't know you like I do, Ivy. I love you, Ivy. I have for a long time." His blue eyes looked at her hard. "You're using this guy to fill a need."

"You're just jealous!" Ivy was furious.

"Of course, I'm jealous! I ought to shake some sense into you before you wreck your life and this fellow's too. You're marrying a fantasy, Ivy. He can't possibly live up to your dreams about him. No man could."

With that, Baxter released her wrists and stalked out of the room toward the front door.

Ivy felt shaken. She started to call him back and then stopped. What nerve! Who did he think he was? Her anger rose as she watched him push through the front gate. Yet, at the same time, that old feeling of being left crept up within her again. Someone else she cared about was walking out of her life—forever.

Ivy filled the next few days with activities so she could keep her mind off what had happened with Baxter. One afternoon, she decided to visit Allison and Aunty Fay to discuss her wedding dress. Only Fay was at home.

"Allison has taken her drawing pad and paint box and gone sketching," Fay said. "Why don't you come in, and I'll show you her designs?"

Ivy followed her into the living room. There on the table lay sheets of paper with various drawings on them.

"With a December wedding, we can use rich materials such as velvet and satin," Fay began. "The way Allison is designing the gown, it will work perfectly."

As they were talking, Ivy heard the back door close and footsteps down the hall.

"Your sketches are beautiful, Allison!" Ivy exclaimed as her friend entered the room.

Allison only replied, "I want it to be a lovely gown."

Something in Allison's tone chilled Ivy. Some sort of barrier had come between them. They were separated in a way they had never been separated before. Ivy felt sad. The thought of losing her deep friendship with Allison was almost more than she could bear. If only Allison would approve of her decision to marry Russell, everything would be all right.

16

Two weeks later Ivy had her first fitting.

"It's a dream dress, Aunty Fay!" Ivy declared as she stepped down from the little platform.

"I hope I can do Allison's design justice," Fay managed to say in spite of the pins in her mouth. "There now, take it off gently so you don't stick yourself."

Ivy slipped out of the bodice and handed it to the seamstress. "It's going to be the loveliest wedding gown any girl ever had. Thank you!"

On her way home, Ivy dawdled. It was a beautiful, golden Indian summer afternoon. She was tempted to stop by the bank and try to get Russ away from his desk to walk with her down by the river. Of course, she knew he wouldn't. He was too responsible ever to do something like that.

Ivy was humming as she walked through the front door of the house. When she stopped at the hall mirror to untie her bonnet ribbons, she heard voices coming from her father's study. Strange, she thought. What was her father doing home at this time of day?

For a heartbeat, she remained absolutely still, listening. Then slowly Ivy turned around and moved across the hall to the study door. She tapped lightly.

"Who is it?"

"It's Ivy, Daddy."

"Come in."

Ivy opened the door and went in. She saw her mother was there and that she had been crying.

Her father patted his wife's shoulder, saying, "This concerns Ivy too, Mercedes. We can't keep this from her. Besides, it'll be all over the papers tomorrow if young Baxter McNeil has anything to say about it."

"Baxter? What does Baxter have to do with it?"

"He's the reporter who broke the story."

"Surely the *Messenger* won't print these accusations against you, Dan. They haven't been proven!"

"That's what I've been trying to tell you. The paper has all the proof. That's why the editor came to me. He wanted me to deny it."

"Daddy, what's happened?" Ivy was getting increasingly alarmed.

Her father sat down in his chair and began to rearrange the inkwell and blotter on his desk. "I've been accused of misconduct as a public official, Ivy. The paper is alleging that I've granted favors to certain contractors regardless of their bids on city projects. It maintains I've been getting money from them in return."

Ivy felt the blood drain from her head as the world came crashing down around her.

The very next day, the scandal broke. GRAND JURY TO INVESTIGATE MAYOR ELLISON FOR WRONG-DOING IN OFFICE, the headline in the morning edition of the *Brookdale Messenger* read.

Late that afternoon, Mayor Ellison shut himself in his study. A short while later, he opened the door. Ivy had just taken some mint tea up to her mother, who had been in bed all day with a headache. "I need to talk to you," he said.

"Ivy, we don't have much time. There are some things you need to know." Her father lowered his voice to a hoarse whisper. "The grand jury's been called to hear testimony against me. They'll move fast."

Ivy's knees felt like water. She sank down on the wingback chair opposite his big desk.

"They'll probably take steps to freeze my bank account so I won't be able to draw out any money," he went on. "I'm sure I'm being watched, or I will be tomorrow at least. So I need for you to do something important for me." He opened a desk drawer and brought out a slim leather case. "In here is a key to our safe-deposit box at the Pemberton Bank." He handed the case to her. "There are several hundred dollars in bills there. I want you to go to the bank and take them out."

Ivy looked at him with questioning eyes.

"This is money my mother left me. You never knew her, Ivy. She died before you came to us. I'd almost forgotten about it until I was going through my desk today. It's not much, but it'll tide you and your mother over in case something happens." He looked at her with sad eyes. "Do you understand?"

Ivy nodded.

Late that evening Russell arrived at the Ellison house, a rolled up newspaper under his arm.

"Oh, Russell, I'm so glad you're here," Ivy said as he threw the paper on the hall table. "How can they print such awful lies about Daddy?" She shuddered. "Let's go into the parlor and sit a while."

Ivy moved toward the fireplace. "This is all so horrible. And it's such a bad time with your folks coming this weekend."

Russell cleared his throat. "Ivy, I don't think this is a good time for my parents to come to Brookdale."

Ivy looked at him. "But Russ, when will I meet them? I know this isn't the best time, but—"

His face got red. "It would be too embarrassing, Ivy. For them and for your father."

Ivy felt as if a sudden draft of icy wind had blown over her. It was a familiar feeling. When had she felt it before? In an instant, she recognized it. The feeling was fear. Fear of being left. Fear of losing everything and everyone. Once more, fear gripped her heart.

"I know you must be tired." Russell's words cut in. "I'd better go."

Ivy wanted to cry out. "Please don't leave me alone! I'm afraid of what's going to happen." She wanted Russell to hold her and tell her everything would be all right. Instead, he walked toward the hall.

"Let me know if I can do anything," he said as he turned to leave. "Good night."

Standing at the edge of the porch steps, Ivy watched him walk briskly into the shadows. Shivering, she went back inside and quickly shut the door.

The story of the mayor's arrest, splashed daily in the papers, had shocked the entire community. Every time Ivy left the house she could feel people staring at her.

When the grand jury indictment came through, the police picked up her father and escorted him to jail to await trial.

Ivy moved through the next few weeks as if she were living a bad dream. Much of her anger was directed toward Baxter McNeil. To think that the man who had once declared his love for her had been a part of this terrible disgrace! The worst thought of all was that her rejection of Baxter may have caused him to do this. Guilt haunted her days and made her sleepless nights more miserable.

More and more, Russell was finding excuses not to visit. He had too much work to do. He was too tired. He had made plans with some friends. He was going out of town for a few days. Ivy really didn't blame him though. She wasn't the best company right now.

Neither was her mother. Mercedes spent most of her days in her bedroom with the curtains drawn. "I don't know what we're going to do, Ivy," she would moan with her hands on her temples and her eyes closed. "There's a lien against all our belongings, and we're going to have to pay your father's lawyer, and—"

Ivy thought about asking Russell, but she knew he wouldn't help. No, this was something she would have to figure out by herself. Old feelings of loneliness and despair seemed to engulf her every thought. She was alone again.

During the trial, Ivy and her mother sat in the packed courtroom. Ivy could barely absorb everything being said. It was almost impossible for her to believe her father had cheated people.

"The testimony is completed now and the jury will retire to deliberate," the judge announced. "Court's in recess until they've reached a verdict." The sound of his gavel on the bench boomed across the room.

"Ivy, could you please get me some water?" Mercedes asked weakly. "I'm not feeling well."

Ivy hurried out of the courtroom into the hallway. She spotted a water cooler at the other end of the hall. She filled two small paper cups with water and was just turning to take them back when she ran straight into Baxter.

"Ivy, I'd like to—"

"Well, if it isn't the star reporter!" Ivy's eyes flashed as she spit out the words. "So how does it feel to be a sneak and prowl around trying to find dirt on someone?"

Baxter's tone was low and calm. "I didn't have to look very far, Ivy. The evidence was all there. Your father didn't try very hard to hide his deals."

"Oh, really? You think people like to be accused of being dishonest? Then try it. I don't believe a word of what you printed about Daddy."

Baxter's voice was steady but strained. "You know better than that. You know I take pride in my integrity. Have you forgotten?"

"Spare me, Baxter McNeil. You've changed. If I didn't despise you so much, I'd feel sorry for you."

Ivy brushed past him and walked into the courtroom. Her hands were still trembling as she handed the half-empty paper cup to her mother.

Later, the bailiff announced that court was once again in session.

"Have you reached a verdict?" the judge asked.

"We have, Your Honor," the jury foreman replied. "We find the defendant guilty as charged."

The days after the verdict passed slowly. Ivy and her mother had been allowed a short time with Dan before he was transferred to the state penitentiary. They didn't know when they would see him again. His sentence was for five to fifteen years. Their grief was too deep for words.

Ivy wandered about the big house, once filled with laughter and activity but now so silent. What would they do now? Mercedes had retreated to her bedroom and remained there. She was no help. Creditors were closing in. The house had to be sold. All their furniture would be auctioned off. They had to find a place to live.

As Ivy's thoughts tortured her, she noticed an envelope on the hall table. The writing was familiar. She ripped it open.

Dear Ivy,

Aunty has written me about the awful thing that has happened. I'm so sorry. I wish I could be there with you. It's hard to be away when your best friend is in trouble. Please go see Aunty. She is such a wonderful person. I know she could be a comfort to you right now.

Always,
Allison

That evening, Ivy dressed with special care for a visit from Russell. They hadn't had a chance to talk in weeks. Now that the trial was over, maybe they could talk about their wedding.

Pulling back the stiff lace curtain, she peered out into the darkness. Winter was almost here, she thought. Where did the fall go?

Just then, she heard a knock on the front door.

"Oh, Russ, I'm so glad to see you!" she exclaimed. "It's been so dreadful. Thank goodness you're here." She took his hand. "I have so much to tell you."

"Let's go into the parlor," Russell said. "I have something important to tell you."

The tone in his voice sounded strange. Puzzled, Ivy said, "Of course."

"I've been offered a position at a bank branch near St. Louis," he began. "This is a golden opportunity, and I can't turn it down." He fingered his silk cravat nervously.

She looked at his eyes. In them she suddenly saw that Russell had no intention of marrying her! Not now, after the scandal. To marry her would ruin his career. Married to the daughter of a convict! Unthinkable! She saw it all in one blinding moment of truth.

"I didn't mean to hurt you, Ivy," Russell stammered.

She held back the tears. "It's all right, Russ. I understand." She turned away. "Now, will you please just go?" Her back to him, Ivy stood frozen.

She heard his footsteps moving across the floor of the parlor and along the hall. A moment later came the sound of the front door closing. Ivy remained standing very straight, every nerve strained.

She had truly believed Russell Trent loved her. Was love so easily ended? Had she been wrong all along? She had been so sure he would protect and care for her. Instead, like all the others, he had abandoned her.

She sank slowly onto the bare floor and buried her face in her hands, sobbing.

Ivy went through the motions of living. She began packing their clothes and looking for a small apartment. As she opened the mail one morning, the doorbell rang.

"I was hoping you'd be home." It was Fay. "I haven't come before because I didn't want to intrude."

"Please come in, Aunty Fay. Mama is resting, but she appreciated the note you sent. It was good of you to write. Not many did."

The expression on Fay's face was kind, her eyes soft. Somehow, the wall Ivy had been building around her emotions suddenly cracked in two. "Oh, Aunty Fay," she sobbed. "I still can't believe someone like Daddy is in prison with real criminals!"

The two sat down on the sofa in the parlor.

"We're often called to bear things we cannot," Fay answered gently. "But you must, Ivy. Not only for your sake, but for your mother's."

Ivy fumbled for the handkerchief in her skirt pocket. "But it's so hard. So much has happened all at once. And on top of everything else, Russell has broken off our engagement." Ivy smiled slightly. "I guess Allison will be glad about that."

Fay put out her hand and covered Ivy's. "She'll be sad that you've been hurt, Ivy. She just didn't think he was right for you."

Ivy shrugged. "I guess he didn't think so either."

"I wish there was something I could do to help you, dear."

"I don't seem to have the strength to face it, Aunty Fay." Ivy lowered her eyes.

"You must ask for it, Ivy. Just enough for each day. That's all any of us has," Fay said. "When I was a young girl, I loved to dance more than anything in the world. And then I had the accident. My leg was so badly crushed the doctors told my parents I'd never walk again, let alone dance. I was in despair. I was crippled and couldn't see any hope for my future."

Fay smiled. Ivy was amazed how her smile lit up her plain face. She was almost beautiful.

"But I was wrong," she continued. "I have a wonderful life. If it hadn't been for the accident, I might never have learned to sew. I've been able to support myself and Allison. And now, I'm married to a wonderful man. I have everything I thought I would never have because of the accident."

"But how did you get through it?" Ivy was hanging on every word.

"I had a loving aunt who taught me something very important. She would write Bible promises on squares of cloth and show me how to embroider them. While I was stitching, I was also learning the verses. Little by little, God's Word was imprinted on my mind and my heart."

Ivy had never prayed very much. "We memorized Scripture verses in Sunday school," she recalled.

"Ask the Lord to bring them to mind. There's nothing mysterious about it. God is eager to help his children. You only have to ask."

Fay stood up. "Now, I really must go, dear."

They walked to the front door.

"Was there one particular verse that helped you, Aunty Fay?" Ivy asked.

She thought a minute. "Joel 2:25: 'I will restore to you the years that the locust hath eaten.' I've watched God do that in my life. If you trust him, you'll see him do it in yours too."

Oh, how she hoped Fay was right.

After Fay left, Ivy opened the mail. One letter was from the state prison. Her father could now receive visitors. She fixed a cup of chamomile tea and went upstairs to tell Mercedes.

Her mother burst into tears. "I can't go, Ivy. I can't see him like that!"

"But Mother, you have to go!" Ivy begged. "Just imagine how lonely Daddy's been, how he's longing to see us. We can't disappoint him. Please!"

The night before their visit, Ivy tossed and turned. At last, the gray dawn light filtered into her bedroom. Before dawn, they were already standing in the station house holding a package of goodies and waiting for the early morning train. Hearing the train whistle as the engine rounded the bend, Ivy felt that old shuddering sensation. She gripped her mother's arm tight until the train pulled to a stop.

A wave of the past swept by her as she helped her mother down the narrow aisle of seats. The smell of coal dust. The sound of clanking and clanging. Even the conductor's voice bellowing directions. Once, so long ago, she had ridden a similar train to this place, the town that had changed her life forever.

The swaying motion of the train lulled Ivy into a strange state. She stared out the window into the dark morning. Gradually, the reflection became that of a little girl, eyes too big for her tiny face. Ivy's mind wandered back over the years. What if she had never traded dresses with Allison? How different things would be.

Ivy pressed her hands tightly together in her lap, suddenly remembering Aunty Fay's visit. "Dear Lord," she prayed, "please help Mother to get through this. Please help *me* to get through this!"

A light drizzle was falling when they got off. In the distance, looming like a crouching monster, a great stone structure overlooked the town. Ivy's throat felt tight. This was it, the place where her daddy was. Squaring her shoulders, she walked inside the station house.

"Sir, could you please tell me how to get to the state prison?" She kept her head held high.

"There's a horse car from the prison. It's outside on the other side of the street," he responded indifferently.

"Thank you."

As the wagon bumped and rocked its way up the winding hill, Ivy looked out the window at the barren hills. This cheerless landscape must be the view from Daddy's tiny cell window. Ivy felt sick. How sad for a man who had once owned such a beautiful home.

"Be back here at three sharp," the driver barked as they got off. "Ain't none till nine if you miss it."

"Prisoners ain't allowed no hard objects," the guard said as he inspected their package and pulled out a pen. "We'll give him this basket later."

"But I wanted to give it to him!" Ivy countered.

"Next!" he yelled as he placed the package to one side.

The visitors' room was a huge area with gunmetal gray walls and high windows. Ivy and her mother sank down on one of the wooden benches along the wall. They heard the grating sound of a bolt sliding back and the twist of keys in the lock. "This way!" a loud male voice called out.

When Ivy saw her father, she pressed one hand to her mouth. He had lost all his healthy ruddy color, and his dark hair was more thickly threaded with gray than she remembered. He looked old and thin.

"Hello, my darlings," he greeted them with a half smile from the other side of the mesh screen separating them. "I'm so glad you've come."

Her mother spent time alone with her father. Afterward, Ivy helped her up from the chair and led her back to the bench against the wall. Then it was Ivy's turn.

"Daddy, we brought you a package," Ivy began. "Oranges and a box of chocolate-covered cherries and your favorite— peppermint drops! But the guard wouldn't let me bring them in. He said they'd give them to you later."

"I'll enjoy them, I'm sure," he replied. Then he leaned closer, his eyes sad. "I don't want you and your mother to visit anymore, Ivy."

Stunned, Ivy protested, "But Daddy, I *want* to come."

He shook his head. "Sweetheart, I'm serving my sentence. I'm getting the punishment I deserve. It has nothing to do with you. It'll be easier for me not to have you come."

Ivy glanced at the other people nearby. Some people were crying. Others were talking quietly, trying to touch one another through the screen.

Her father continued. "It may be hard for you to believe now, but the time will pass. Five years isn't forever. One day this will be over."

"But Daddy—"

He held up a hand. "Hear me out, Ivy. I've had a lot of time to think about this. I see the mistakes I've made. When I get out of here, things are going to be different. With God's help, I'm going to be different too." He smiled. "So I want you to take care of your mother, my dear. I'm sorry it's going to be up to you, but I know you've got what it takes."

Ivy was almost too choked up to whisper good-bye as she put both her hands on the mesh screen separating them, touching his palms.

With a saddened heart Ivy left him that day. She had no idea when she would see him again. Five years seemed like a lifetime to her.

19

HELP WANTED: Sales Clerk. Ivy was passing Fallons' Mercantile early one morning when she spotted the sign in the front window. She paused then walked quickly by.

During the weeks since visiting her father, a great deal had happened. Their house and furniture had all been sold. She and her mother had found a small furnished apartment in an older section of Brookdale. There was still two hundred dollars left from Grandma Ellison, but Ivy knew this wouldn't last long. She had to find a job.

She had searched the newspapers and circled want ads. She had answered them with letters and even personal visits. Over and over her hopes had been dashed. The reason given was that she did not have the experience needed. Ivy believed it was more than that. The name Ellison had been tarnished. No one wanted to hire someone with this name. Fallons' Mercantile was the last place in the world Ivy wanted to work. But she needed a job desperately. And it *was* a job.

Ivy circled the block. Her dislike of Mrs. Fallon battled with her need. To walk in there and ask for employment would be humiliating. But she had to make a decision. It was nine o'clock and the store had just opened.

People go to work every day, she told herself sternly. I can do this. Why, I even remember the circus people who worked so hard. Suddenly, Sophia's remarks about the "freaks" surfaced in her mind. "Who else would hire someone like them?" Sophia had asked. Ivy thought, Who will hire someone like me?

She prayed. "Lord, like Aunty Fay said, I need enough strength for today. Your Word says you will provide. We need your provision—and soon."

As she buttoned her jacket, she discovered it was loose. She had lost weight in the past few weeks. She hoped she didn't look too thin. She brushed back her hair and tucked in the wisps of curls that kept escaping from under her bonnet brim. "There now," she encouraged herself. "Off to conquer the enemy!" She braced herself and pushed open the half-glass front door.

Wilbur Fallon was standing behind the counter. When he heard the front bell, his eyes stared at her through the thick lenses of his glasses.

Ivy found her voice. "Good day, Mr. Fallon. I understand you're looking for a clerk."

Almost from the minute she removed the HELP WANTED sign the next morning, Mrs. Fallon began rattling off a list of duties for Ivy.

"You're not going to any fancy tea party here, Miss Ellison," she said, giving Ivy a smug look. She tossed Ivy a coarse, brown cotton coverall. "This is what clerks wear." With that, she pointed to the broom and feather duster.

"The floor has to be swept and all the counters dusted before we open the doors. Now, get to work!"

That first day, Mrs. Fallon followed Ivy around talking constantly, like a snapping turtle. She would jab a finger at a corner Ivy had missed or run her fingertips along the edge of a display case to pick up some leftover dust. When six o'clock finally came, Ivy was exhausted.

Wearily she put on her hat and prepared to leave.

"You understand that we're looking for a clerk with experience." Mrs. Fallon jangled her keys in one hand, waiting to lock up. "So, we're hiring you temporarily until we see how you do. And, of course, it'll be a while before we let you wait on customers. We take pride in the goodwill of this community, you know."

Ivy could feel every acid drop of the woman's sarcasm.

Ivy woke up early each morning, tiptoed past her mother's bedroom and out to the kitchen. When the kettle whistled, Ivy poured boiling water into a small percolator for coffee. By the time the hands of the clock pointed to eight, she was dressed and ready to leave.

Usually she left coffee on the back of the stove and some sliced toast for her mother. Then she would put on her hat and coat, tug on her gloves, and hurry downstairs. It took about fifteen minutes to walk into town, and she didn't want to be late. She could just imagine Mrs. Fallon's attitude if she walked in even one minute after 8:30.

As the days went on, Ivy eagerly completed most of her chores by midday and was left with very little to do. At last, Mrs. Fallon decided to let her wait on a few customers.

"But first," she sneered, "you have to memorize our inventory. We take care of our customers here. They need to feel they can rely on us. You'll need to be able to pull something from the shelf as soon as someone asks about it."

Ivy determined to accept the challenge. Within a few weeks, she had mastered the list.

This didn't stop Mrs. Fallon. When the store wasn't crowded, she assigned Ivy the most unpleasant tasks. The one the new clerk disliked the most was carrying stock up to the attic. She had to climb a wobbly ladder and push open the trapdoor in the ceiling. The unfinished loft was dark with warped planks and excess stock stacked everywhere. She would often come back down with spider webs caught in her hair and her face smudged with dust. It seemed like Mrs. Fallon took pleasure in giving Ivy this chore.

One time, she ordered Ivy to take up some large cardboard cartons Mr. Fallon had brought back from the freight depot. The thing Ivy hated most was climbing the ladder. She had never really gotten over her fear of heights since that time she'd climbed the rope with Liselle. She always tried to remember Liselle's rules though: Don't panic, don't look down, and God will take care of the rest.

As she carried two boxes into the back room, however, she found Mr. Fallon preparing to take three boxes of new fabric up to storage.

"Mr. Fallon," she said, "Mrs. Fallon would like these put up in the attic right away."

"Well, just put 'em down. I'll get 'em on my second trip," he grunted.

"Would you like me to hold the ladder while you go up?" she asked. "I've noticed it's rather unsteady."

He nodded his head yes and planted the ladder beneath the trapdoor. His arms loaded, he began to climb while Ivy gripped the sides. When he was halfway up, Ivy realized that one of the rungs was now coming loose.

"One of these rungs is loose, Mr. Fallon," she called out. "We might need to fix it later."

"Wanta hand up those cartons?" He seemed to ignore her words. "I need to get this done."

Day after day, Ivy wearily got up and went off to work. Mr. Fallon didn't seem to dislike her. In fact, at one point he even gave her a key to the front door. "In case of an emergency," he had told her as he locked up one night. However, Mrs. Fallon remained spiteful and harsh. Ivy determined to stay pleasant and willing to help. And as she did, something began happening inside her. Whatever she had to put up with, she told herself, was the price she had to pay to keep her promise to her father. As mean-spirited as Mrs. Fallon was, this was a job. It kept a roof over their heads and food on the table.

Slowly but surely, Ivy began to realize she could survive. She had lived through Greystone and the circus. She had weathered abandonment more than once. She had faced her father's disgrace. Over and over as she worked at the store, Sophia's words returned to her soul. *Whatever you are inside is what counts.* Ivy was getting to the point of understanding that what others think doesn't really matter. Maybe she was growing up after all. No matter what Mrs. Fallon did, Ivy decided she was not going to let the shopkeeper change her heart.

20

The spring of 1899 came, but Ivy hardly noticed. Her days were long and hard. At night when she walked home from work, she was too tired to notice the blossoms on the trees. On Sundays, she had too many things to do to get ready for the next week's work.

One Saturday evening, Ivy sat down to write a letter to her father. As she wrote the date, she realized she had been working at the store for three months. Ivy dipped her pen in the inkwell and began:

Dear Daddy,

You will be glad to know Mother is doing fine. She is sleeping better at night and working on her needlepoint during the day.

Ivy paused. This wasn't really the truth. Her mother looked white and drawn, years older than her age of forty-two. Most of the time Mercedes stared vacantly out the window. Only once in a while, when Ivy insisted, she might pick up some needlepoint or go out for a walk. Ivy couldn't bring herself to tell her father how depressed her mother really was, so she didn't.

Ivy did not write about her fears either. However, she did confide in Aunty Fay. Since Allison was still at the Art Institute, Ivy began visiting Fay on Sundays when her mother was resting. Mostly, Fay listened while Ivy poured out her heart about her mother and the job at the mercantile. Ivy soon realized the depth of Fay's faith, and so she heeded her advice. "Pray, Ivy," she would say.

Ivy began to pray. She had never really prayed very much. She had seen the Fortunatos cross themselves and caught Liselle reading her Bible from time to time. She had attended Sunday school with the Ellisons, but she'd never developed a sincere prayer life of her own. Oh, maybe she tossed a few prayers here and there up to heaven, hoping God would catch them. But she never believed the Lord would answer. The guilt of her lies and the feeling she was not worthy made Ivy feel that God wasn't going to listen anyway.

One day while Ivy was visiting Fay, she learned that Allison would soon be coming home for the summer.

"She's won some awards and even another year's scholarship!" Fay told her as she poured a cup of tea.

Sunlight streamed through the light curtains onto the floor.

"That's great, Aunty Fay," Allison replied. "I really do miss her!"

"So do I," Fay echoed.

Ivy wished she could meet her friend at the train station, but Mrs. Fallon wouldn't let her off work. Ivy planned to join the family for a welcome home dinner instead.

"Come in!" Allison exclaimed. "I'm so glad to see you! It seems like ages since last summer."

With their arms around each other, the two went inside. Good smells floated from the back of the house. In the kitchen, Fay's husband, Matthew, was sitting in a rocking chair reading a paper.

"How good to see you, Ivy. Everything's just about ready."

The table was covered with a pale blue woven cloth and set with Fay's blue and white Danish stoneware. Soon a platter of golden fried chicken and bowls of fluffy potatoes, baked yams, and fresh salad were placed on it. Fay had made a special strawberry shortcake for the occasion.

After they had finished, Allison spoke up. "Now, Aunty, Ivy and I will clear away the dishes."

Fay hesitated.

"You go on and finish that dress you're working on."

Matthew politely excused himself to smoke his pipe out on the back porch, and Fay walked into the next room.

As soon as the two friends were alone, Allison squeezed Ivy's arm. "Oh, Ivy, I have something so exciting to tell you. I can hardly believe it myself!" Allison's eyes shone like stars.

"I'm in love!" she exclaimed in the next breath.

"Who is he?" Ivy begged.

"I haven't even told Aunty yet. But she'll meet him soon. He's coming here the third week in June when he's finished his work at the institute."

Allison picked up the empty platter of fried chicken, now covered with crumbs. "You see, he's an instructor there. A fine artist. And he's the kindest, most intelligent, dearest man I've ever known. I can't wait for you to meet him."

Ivy set down the stack of plates she was carrying. "Wait a minute. Slow down! He's an instructor? Isn't he a lot older than you then?"

"No, not really. He's only thirty-two, one of the youngest teachers there actually." Allison twirled around in a small circle. "Oh, Ivy, I never dreamed such a thing could happen to me!"

Ivy hugged her. "Of course it could. You deserve all the happiness of anyone, Allison." And Ivy meant it.

The two friends sat down on the high kitchen stools, dawdling over the dishes.

"His name is Roger Benson," Allison began. "I took several classes with him, and he's been so encouraging. He does watercolors and has exhibited in some local galleries."

"Not done yet?" Fay's voice from the other room brought them back to the present.

Ivy glanced at the kitchen clock. "Oh my, it's nearly nine o'clock." She jumped down from the stool. "I told Mother I wouldn't be late."

"How's your mother?" Allison's eyes were concerned.

"She isn't herself yet, and I'm not sure she'll pull out of it until Daddy comes home."

"Give her my best, Ivy," Allison remarked sincerely.

"I will," Ivy replied as she picked up her jacket and hat.

Roger Benson arrived the third week in June. He rented a room in a nearby guest house but became almost a permanent member of the Lund household. The couple took off on day-long drawing trips or sketching expeditions. Before he left in August, he had won over the Lunds and asked for Allison's hand in marriage. The Lunds readily gave their approval.

Ivy tried not to be jealous, but she was. Roger was taking up almost all of Allison's time, so Ivy rarely saw her. When he finally left, it was already time for Allison to begin packing to return to St. Louis herself. This would be her final semester at the Art Institute. Although a definite wedding date had not yet been set, Ivy realized their lives would soon be forever changed.

After Allison left, Ivy struggled with loneliness and sadness. She had lost so many important people in her life. She had known the grief of losing her father, her home, and her fiancé within a few short months.

She had also thought she knew what love was until she had seen Allison with Roger. Had she loved Russell that way? She thought she had, but she now realized it wasn't true. Russell had been selfish and self-centered. Roger wasn't at all like that. Russell would never have made her happy. Even Baxter had seen that. Ivy had to admit that maybe Baxter had been right after all.

21

During the warm, sunny days in September, Ivy frequently spent her lunch hour at a park near the store. The trees dotting the sweeping grass painted a glorious picture against the clear, cloudless blue sky. This time was a refreshing part of her difficult days at the mercantile. It gave her time to think, and she began realizing that being alone wasn't so bad after all.

One particular noon, Ivy had just checked her watch. Lunch hour was nearly over. She hopped up and walked down to the edge of the pond where she scattered the remains of her sandwich on the water for the ducks. Just as she turned around, she saw a tall familiar figure striding down the sidewalk. Baxter McNeil!

She had not seen Baxter since that awful day in the courthouse. She was ashamed of how she had acted back then. What should she do? Turn and run or face him?

At about the same time, Baxter saw her. He slowed down but kept on walking. As he neared, he took off his hat. "Ivy," he murmured.

"Hello, Baxter." Ivy swallowed hard. "I owe you an apology."

"No, Ivy, it's I—"

"Baxter," she interrupted. "I was wrong to accuse you of lying. My father believes you were just doing your job. And I do too, now."

"Don't say any more," he replied. "I understand. I'm only sorry you were hurt."

"No one gets through life without being hurt. I've done my share of hurting other people too." Ivy brushed some bread crumbs off her hands. "I hurt you. And I'm sorry."

"Maybe this isn't the time or place, but would it be possible for us to talk?"

"I don't think that's a good idea, Baxter. I'm at the store six days a week until six o'clock. I try to spend my evenings with Mother. She isn't well."

"I'm sorry."

"I have to get back to work. I'm glad we ran into one another."

Later that evening, Ivy realized that seeing Baxter had touched something deep within her. She had acted horribly to him that day at the courthouse, and she was glad she had apologized. It was true that Baxter had only been doing his job, and as awful as it was, Ivy had finally accepted her father's guilt.

As she sat on the sofa near her mother, Ivy discovered how free she suddenly felt. It was a relief to have asked for forgiveness. It was freeing to know she had set things right with Baxter. It was so much better to bring things into the light.

The following Sunday Ivy walked over to see Fay.

"You must have known I was thinking about you," Fay declared as she welcomed Ivy. "Yesterday I got a letter from Allison. Roger has accepted a teaching position at a school back East. He has to report immediately, so they want to be married right away."

A stunned Ivy followed Fay into the kitchen.

"Of course, she wants you to be her maid of honor." Fay was putting the kettle on the stove. "I'll have to get busy on the dresses."

That night, the first winter rain fell. Ivy knew it was the end of the lovely Indian summer. As she listened to the tiny raindrops pounding the roof, memories flooded her soul. A year ago her future had seemed bright and exciting. She had just finished Elmhurst and was engaged to Russell. What would her future be like now?

She remembered the time she had pointed to Sophia's crystal ball and asked, "Can you really see the future?" Sophia's dark eyes had narrowed. "Nobody can see into the future, Ivy," she had said. "And if they could, they wouldn't want to." Ivy had dreamed about a future of sunshine and happiness. Now it seemed veiled in darkness. What kind of world would she know working at Fallons' Mercantile for the rest of her life?

Ivy sat down on the edge of the couch and put her head in her hands. She couldn't think about this anymore. She owed her parents for everything they had done for her. She would take care of her mother as long as she was needed. Even if her father had to serve only the minimum sentence of five years, she would do what she had to do. Five years seemed like a lifetime away.

The idea came to Ivy quite suddenly. The day after Allison got home, Ivy went to see her.

"There's something I need to talk to you about, Allison," Ivy began.

"Of course. Let's go into the kitchen."

Ivy knew Fay was busy sewing in the next room. "We need to talk privately. Could we take a walk and go down to the river?"

Allison stopped in the hall and turned around. "Is something wrong?"

"I hope not. That is, I hope it can be set straight."

Puzzled, Allison quickly told Fay where they were going.

Walking along the graveled path, the two friends strolled through the gate and down the road toward the river.

"So, what's so important?" Allison prodded as she linked her arm in Ivy's.

Ivy felt a knot form in the pit of her stomach. How would Allison react to the news? Would she be angry? Would she be able to forgive?

"Allison, I have a confession to make. I've done something terrible to you."

"What do you mean?" Allison stopped walking and looked at her friend. "You're my best friend, Ivy. You always have been."

"Wait until you hear what I have to tell you." Ivy gently removed her friend's arm. "Remember when we came here on the Orphan Train?"

Allison nodded.

"Well, I did something that was very wrong."

Allison was frowning now.

"I thought going to the Ellisons was the best thing that ever happened to me."

"And it was, wasn't it?" her friend broke in. "They both love you very much, and for so long they were able to give you whatever you wanted."

"That's just it, Allison," Ivy's voice trembled. "All that *should* have happened to *you*. It should have been *you!*"

"I don't know what you're talking about, Ivy."

"Don't you remember? Just before the train came into Brookdale, we traded dresses?"

Ivy smiled. "Sure, that cute little plaid suit you were wearing and—"

"And I put on your flowered dress with the lace collar. It had *your* name, 'Allison,' sewn on the hem. Mrs. Willoughby got us mixed up. She looked at the name on the hem and thought it spelled *Ellison*. We went to the wrong families!"

Tears spilled down Ivy's cheeks. "Oh, Allison, I'm so sorry! Can you ever forgive me?"

The look on Allison's face was totally blank, her eyes wide open.

"Don't you see?" Ivy stumbled on. "I traded lives with you, Allison. You would have been able to have all the advantages I had—with the Ellisons. Clothes, trips, education. I cheated you. If I'd spoken up that day . . ." Ivy put her hands over her face and began to sob.

The next thing she felt was Allison's arms going around her shaking shoulders. "It's all right, Ivy. It doesn't matter now. It's all worked out." Allison handed Ivy a handkerchief so she could wipe her eyes and blow her nose.

"Do you hate me?" Ivy asked.

"Of course not. It was all meant to be. I've had a wonderful life, Ivy. Aunty couldn't have given me more love and devotion. I've been so blessed. Please don't worry. There's nothing to forgive."

They held each other, and after a while, Ivy's tears stopped. With their arms still around each other's waists, they walked slowly back toward the house. Ivy felt closer to Allison than she had ever felt before. The secret was out at last. Confession was good for the soul.

That night at home, Ivy felt enormous relief. Her prayers came from her heart, and she felt clean. Her spirit was free. Tears came again, but these were different tears, like a spring thaw after a frozen winter. She wept for the frightened little girl who had been forced to live all these years with the weight of such guilt. At last it was gone.

Calm now, Ivy realized there was one more thing she wanted to do. She opened the lid of the trunk in the corner. A smell of crushed rose petals and lavender reached her nose. She lifted out a muslin garment bag and unfastened it. There, in all its original beauty, was the wedding dress Fay had made for her.

It was only right that this should be Allison's. After all, she had created it, and Fay had fashioned it. In some symbolic way, Ivy would be giving back to her what she had taken away so long ago—a dress.

22

Allison's wedding was planned for noon on a Saturday. That morning, Ivy put on the new dress Fay had made for her. Just before leaving, she grabbed her small beaded bag, hat, and pink silk gloves. "See you tonight, Mother," she called as she rushed through the door.

Mrs. Fallon would not let her off even without pay, so Ivy was not able to be Allison's bridesmaid. But she was determined to complete all her chores in the morning so she could get to the church on time for the ceremony. As soon as she arrived at the mercantile, she donned the clerk's overall apron and got to work.

About 11:15 the bell above the door jangled. A woman with a large hat and feather boa swished into the store. Mrs. Fallon greeted her. After a few moments, she escorted the woman over to Ivy.

"Our clerk will be happy to help you select what you want, Mrs. Cates." Mrs. Fallon turned to Ivy with a smirk on her face. "Mrs. Cates has just moved to Brookdale, Miss Ellison. Her husband is the new assistant cashier at the Brookdale Savings and Loan."

The news jolted Ivy. This was the wife of Russell's replacement!

"I want to see some gloves," the woman directed.

"Any particular kind? Leather, kid, silk?" Ivy forced herself to think about the task at hand.

"Just show me what you have, something dressy," Mrs. Cates replied.

Ivy brought out various gloves, taking them out of their narrow boxes and displaying them for the woman to see. Mrs. Cates carelessly tossed each pair on the counter before picking up another. Ivy tried to keep track of which gloves went in which box.

At ten minutes to noon, Mrs. Cates flung down a pair of dove gray gloves. "I suppose these will do," she finally decided. "Wrap them up for me. I'll take them."

Ivy quickly boxed the gloves, wrote out the sales ticket, and politely directed the customer to the cash register. Then she hurriedly put the discarded gloves back into their boxes and returned them to the shelf. While Mrs. Fallon was ringing up the purchase, Ivy dashed into the back room.

"Don't forget," Mrs. Fallon stuck her head in the door and said sharply, "Mr. Fallon's gone over to Bridgeport. I can't spare you more'n an hour."

"I know, Mrs. Fallon," Ivy replied as she pulled on her gloves, picked up her bag, and hurried out the back door.

Ivy could hear the organ music as she reached the church steps. She had just removed her gloves when the organist struck the opening bars of the wedding march. A low murmur flowed through the church as the bride entered. On Matthew's arm, Allison moved gracefully up the aisle toward the altar, where Roger was waiting. When she passed Ivy, she smiled.

The ceremony was short. As the couple started back down the aisle, Allison stopped at the front pew on the left to embrace Fay. Then she drew a rose from her bouquet and handed it to her. The couple proceeded down the aisle again but stopped next to Ivy.

"Dear Ivy," Allison whispered with a hug. Then she drew out another rose and gave it to Ivy. Ivy's eyes were so misted she could hardly see Allison's face.

Ivy made her way through the joyful scene outside the church and headed back to the mercantile. She had gone only a short distance when she heard her name.

"Ivy, you're not going to the reception?" Baxter was hurrying to catch up with her.

"I can't. Saturdays are too busy at the store. I couldn't get the time off."

"I should really get back to the paper myself. May I walk with you?"

Ivy smiled. "Why not?" she replied as he fell into step beside her.

The couple walked a short while, then Baxter broke the silence.

"Ivy, would it be possible for me to call on you some evening?"

"I don't think so, Baxter. We have only a small flat. It would be awkward."

"Then maybe we could go for a drive some Sunday."

Ivy stopped walking and turned to face him. "I know you're trying to be kind, Baxter, but you don't have to. Things are different for me now, for all of us. I think it would be foolish to think we could pick up where we left off."

"I'm not trying to do that, Ivy. I'd like to start over again. Couldn't we?"

Baxter's blue eyes looked at her longingly.

"I don't know."

"Will you at least think about it? I'd very much like to talk."

Suddenly Ivy realized the time. "Oh, Baxter, I've got to go!" She walked briskly away. At the corner, she picked up her skirt and started to run.

"Ivy, wait!" was all she heard, but she couldn't turn back or stop now. Mrs. Fallon would be furious if she was late getting back. And Ivy could not afford to lose this job.

That evening, she placed her single rose into a crystal bud vase on the table and gave her mother a full description of Allison's wedding. "It was beautiful, Mother," she said as they ate dinner. "Simple and lovely, just the way Allison wanted it."

Thoughts of the wedding day brought Baxter McNeil to mind. It had been strange to see him again. He seemed different, more gentle and thoughtful. And he wanted to see her again. Did they have too much history? Had there been too much hurt?

A short while later, Ivy was putting away the clothes she had worn to the wedding. She was emptying her purse when she realized that her gloves were missing. She must have left them on the pew at the church. She made a mental note to check with the church custodian to see if anyone had turned them in.

On Sunday, a warm, sunny day with a crispness in the air, Ivy suggested to her mother that they take a walk over to the park. The trees were mostly bare, but the sun shone brightly on the sparkling surface of the pond. They strolled along the paths and sat down to rest on a bench where they could watch the children sailing toy boats and rolling hoops. Eventually the shadows lengthened over the grass and the sun began to fade.

"I suppose we'd better go, Mother," Ivy said.

Mercedes shook her head. "Not yet, dear. I have something to say." She laid a thin hand on Ivy's wrist. "Ivy, I've failed you."

Ivy was shocked. "Don't say that, Mother."

"I'm so sorry, sweetheart. I've been so depressed, and I've let you carry the load of working and taking care of me all by yourself. I've been weak and foolish." Mercedes squeezed Ivy's wrist. "From now on things are going to be different."

Ivy's heart swelled with thankfulness. Maybe God was listening to her prayers after all.

The next day she walked through the chilly morning to work. Upon entering the store, she saw Mrs. Fallon standing in front of the counter by the cash register. Ivy could tell instantly that she was angry about something.

"Well, Miss Ellison, I assume you're prepared to pay for the merchandise you took on Saturday."

Ivy stared blankly at her. "I don't know what you mean, Mrs. Fallon."

"Oh, no?" Her steely eyes glared at Ivy. "Don't play dumb with me. I'm not stupid. Thought you could get away with it, didn't you? Thought I wouldn't check."

Mrs. Fallon held out an empty glove box. "I found this empty box placed among the other boxes containing gloves. How do you explain that?"

"I don't understand, Mrs. Fallon. The only gloves I sold on Saturday were to Mrs. Cates. I boxed those and you rang them up. I don't know about any others."

Mrs. Fallon's face twisted. "There's a pair of cream doeskin six-button gloves missing, Miss Ellison. Just the kind one might wear to a fancy wedding—"

Ivy felt sick. She tried to keep her voice even. "I wore my own gloves Saturday, Mrs. Fallon. Pale pink silk ones. I purchased them in St. Louis over a year ago. They still have the store tag on the inside."

Mrs. Fallon's mouth curled. "Can you show them to me, Miss Ellison, as proof?"

"Of course—" Just as she spoke, she remembered. Her gloves were missing!

A look of smug satisfaction crossed Mrs. Fallon's face. "Just as I thought! You can't produce them, can you? The ones you wore Saturday were the ones you stole!" Mrs. Fallon threw the empty box on the counter. "Consider yourself dismissed. I'll take the price of the gloves off what money you have coming to you. You're lucky I don't turn you in to the police," she sneered. "Like father, like daughter, I always say."

Anger boiled up inside, ready to explode. But Ivy refused to stoop to Mrs. Fallon's level. Without a word, she turned around and walked out the door.

It wasn't until she was several blocks away that she reacted. Her hands were shaking and her palms were sweaty. She could feel the moisture on her forehead. She felt bruised as though Mrs. Fallon's words had flogged her with a whip.

If I were going to steal anything, it certainly wouldn't be a pair of fancy gloves, she fumed.

She had lost her job. This meant that their income was gone. What was she going to do? She would have to find another job. But where? And how?

She found herself walking toward the park trying to calm herself. Be strong, Ivy, she told herself. Remember Liselle's words: Don't panic. God will take care of the rest. Ivy thought about Fay, who always encouraged her to pray. She needed to pray now.

Gradually she calmed down. As she sat on the bench near the pond, she was hardly aware of the other people. It was only when the sun went behind a cloud and the wind grew cool that Ivy realized the day had passed.

That evening Ivy found Mercedes dressed and waiting for her. She had set the table and baked a meat loaf and roasted potatoes for dinner.

"See? I told you things were going to be different, didn't I?" She smiled at Ivy.

Ivy put on her most cheerful face. Her mother was getting better. Ivy just couldn't take the chance that news of her job would propel her mother back into depression, so she kept quiet.

After Mercedes went to bed, Ivy took out the newspaper and started searching the help wanted section. She looked up and down the columns but found nothing. She was just folding the paper when she heard a knock at the door.

"Baxter!" she gasped when she opened the door.

"Evening, Ivy. I hope you don't mind my dropping by like this, but you were in such a hurry the other day, you didn't hear me. You dropped these." He held out her missing pink gloves.

Ivy couldn't help herself. She burst out laughing. Yes, she could prove to Mrs. Fallon that she wasn't a thief, but did it really matter?

"What's so funny?" he asked.

"Come in, and I'll tell you all about it," she finally managed to say.

When Ivy finished the story, Baxter said, "You're in luck, Ivy. The classified department at the paper is looking for someone. The person will take in ads and help people write them. It's not difficult, and it pays fairly well." He paused. "Probably better than the Fallons paid you."

Ivy smiled. "Well, then, I'll apply tomorrow."

23

The wind was chilly as she left the newspaper building the next day after filling out an application for the job. Ivy bent her head against the wind and shivered. But her mind wasn't on the weather. What was she going to do? She still had the key to the Fallons' store. Mrs. Fallon had already accused her of stealing once. Ivy didn't want her to find grounds to do it again. Ivy had a paycheck coming. She hoped the storekeeper wouldn't try to keep it from her.

Worried and cold, Ivy decided to walk down to the duck pond. By the time she had circled it twice, she knew what she had to do. She would place the key in an envelope and, after closing time, slip it under the front door of the store. The Fallons would find it when they opened for business the next morning. This way, she wouldn't have to face Mrs. Fallon again.

Now, all she needed was an excuse to go out after supper. Without realizing it, her mother provided one.

"I just finished my latest book," Mercedes told her after they had finished eating. "It was a good one. I think I'd like to try a mystery next."

Ivy jumped at the chance. "Why don't I go to the library tonight and pick up a few novels for us both?" She pushed back her chair and picked up her empty plate. "I've finished mine too."

"I'll clean up while you go," Mercedes offered. "The book is on the sofa."

Ivy gathered her jacket and hat and the two books. "I won't be long."

Smoky gray clouds had just begun to roll across the sky. It smelled like rain. Ivy knew she would have to hurry. A block from the store, she could feel her anger rising again. The closer she got to the building, the stronger her resentment grew. She had worked for the Fallons for almost a year. Mr. Fallon had seemed pleased with her work. But nothing was ever good enough for his wife.

Ivy bundled her scarf around her neck as she walked. She thought about all the times she had unpacked boxes of new stock. If she had been a thief, she would have had plenty of opportunities before this. How dare that woman accuse her of stealing!

At the corner, Ivy halted. Her chest felt tight, her stomach painfully knotted. With the books tucked securely under her arm, she drew in a deep breath, reached in her purse for the envelope, and crossed the road.

As she bent down to wedge it under the double door, something caught her attention. Through the glass, she could see a dim light from way in the back. This was odd. Ivy had never known the Fallons to work late. It was nearly eight o'clock. Who could it be?

Ivy hesitated. Part of her wanted just to leave the envelope and go. Yet, her conscience wouldn't let her. What if the Fallons had left a lamp burning in the back? The store might catch on fire. The light bothered her. Ivy simply couldn't turn away.

The wind was picking up now. She would have to make up her mind fast. Maybe she could just quickly peek in and check. It shouldn't take very long. Then she could head on to the library.

She tore open the envelope and unlocked the door. The door hinges creaked as she opened the half-glass door. Shadows lurked along the floor. Quietly, she closed the door behind her. The store was eerie. The wood planks squeaked under her weight as she crept toward the back.

Then she heard it. At first it sounded like the distant moo of a cow. A cold feeling gripped her. She stopped. Then she heard it again. It was a moan. Ivy placed her purse and the books on the counter as she stole forward. There it was again. Ivy hoped her heart didn't sound as loud on the outside as it did on the inside.

Now she could see pale light through the curtains of the storage room. She stepped forward. "Is anyone there?" Her voice was shaky.

"Help—"

Had she heard it right? Barely above a whisper, the voice spoke the word. "Help—"

This time she could hear it better. Someone needed help!

Ivy drew back the curtains. Circles flickered around the room.

"Help, please."

The words came from the back near the attic storage room. The flame sputtered as Ivy picked up the lamp and held it high. There in the corner under the open trapdoor lay a crumpled figure. It was Mrs. Fallon!

"Mrs. Fallon, it's me, Ivy," she said as she crouched down beside her.

"Oh, Ivy," she groaned. "I fell. The ladder broke. My ankle."

Her face was chalky and she was obviously in great pain.

"Don't move." Ivy set the oil lamp down beside her. "Let me see if I can get this off."

The ladder had fallen on top of the woman. It was old and heavy. Sharp splinters stuck out of its rungs. Ivy tugged it, managing to push it over to one side.

"Please, I've been here for hours." Mrs. Fallon was almost wailing now.

Scrambling to her feet, Ivy saw a blanket on top of one of the boxes. She grabbed it and tucked it around Mrs. Fallon. Then she quickly undid her petticoat, stepped out of it, and folded it into a soft pillow.

"I'll go get help," she said as she gently lifted the woman's head. "I'll come back as soon as I can."

Mrs. Fallon nodded weakly then grabbed Ivy's wrist. "Ivy, I took a lamp up in the attic with me when I went. It's still up there." She closed her eyes a moment before continuing. "It's been burning a long time."

Ivy's heart sank. The attic! She would have to climb the rickety ladder herself! All her old fears gripped her. How she hated heights! Could she do this? There was no way out. She would have to overcome the fear she'd had ever since she was a little girl.

"Don't panic," she told herself.

Ivy slid the ladder over until it was under the trap-door. Slowly she lifted it in place. She spotted the missing rung and knew she would have to be careful. Slowly she began to climb.

"Don't look down," Liselle's voice echoed in her ears.

When she reached the top, she pulled herself up. The light from the lamp sent hideous forms across the dark eaves. To her horror, she realized that Mrs. Fallon had set the lamp in an eave on one side. The loft had no real floor. It was just wooden planks set across thin plywood. One false step and she would plummet through to the ground below!

Ivy held her breath. Not since her days in the circus with Paulo had she felt so frightened. But there was no escape. She had to do this.

"Dear God," she prayed silently, "I need your help."

Slowly but surely she placed one foot out to feel the plank. She shifted her weight onto it. Then she did it again on the next plank. When she reached the lamp, she grasped one of the cross posts to steady herself and slowly leaned down to pick it up. The lamp almost slipped in the sweat of her hands, but she held on to it. Then she inched her way back.

"Thank you, Lord," she whispered as she set it down near the trapdoor.

When she reached the bottom of the ladder, Ivy wiped her brow. She had done it! She blew out the smoking lamp and set it on a crate. Mrs. Fallon had not moved.

"I'm going for help," Ivy told her. "I'll go as fast as I can."

Where should she go? She dashed out the double doors onto the porch. The wind was howling in the dark. A storm was coming. Ivy looked up and down the street. There, at the end she saw a light. It was coming from the *Messenger*.

Of course! They would be putting the morning edition of the newspaper together. Ivy ran through the square and up the steps of the redbrick building. People wearing green eyeshades sat at their desks. And there was Baxter.

"Baxter!" she said as she flung open the door. "You've got to come. Something's happened to Mrs. Fallon."

24

Ivy stayed beside Mrs. Fallon while the doctor examined her.

"It looks like you've got a fractured ankle," he told her, as he stood up. "I don't see anything else very serious." The doctor stuffed his stethoscope in his black bag. "Baxter, would you send for the ambulance to take her to the hospital?"

Baxter nodded and walked out.

The doctor turned toward Ivy. "You can stay here, can't you, until the ambulance arrives?"

"Yes, sir."

"Good." The man looked at her kindly. "You prevented her from going into shock, Ivy. Good for you." With that, he stepped through the curtains separating the back room from the store and left.

Mrs. Fallon still lay on the floor. Ivy knelt down beside her.

"Ivy," she moistened her dry lips, "I owe you an apology."

Ivy had never heard Mrs. Fallon utter those words in her life.

"I accused you wrongly about the gloves." Her voice was still weak. "Mrs. Cates came in and told me. She found another pair underneath hers in the box. It was a mistake."

Strangely, Ivy felt neither satisfaction nor relief. She had not stolen the gloves. But now the fact that she had been accused of stealing did not seem to matter. Perhaps it had been her mistake, hurrying to get to the wedding, but at least the matter was settled.

"It's all right, Mrs. Fallon."

The woman cleared her throat. "I just wanted you to know," her voice trailed off.

Before long, the hospital attendants arrived with a stretcher. They placed the injured woman on it and carried her out to the waiting ambulance. Baxter waited with Ivy. After the ambulance had left, the pair made sure the store was secure then went out the front door and locked it.

"You were very brave, Ivy," Baxter said as he gave the handle an extra twist.

"I'm not so sure. I was scared to death."

"But you did it anyway. That's what real courage is, you know."

Baxter surprised her by taking both her hands in his. When she winced, he turned them over. Her palms were scratched from the rough wood of the ladder. "You hurt yourself," he said softly.

She tried to withdraw her hands, but Baxter raised them slowly and kissed them. "Did I ever tell you how much I admire you?" he asked.

Ivy shook her head and pulled her hands away. "Don't give me credit I don't deserve, Baxter," she replied. "If you knew how much I disliked Mrs. Fallon—"

"That doesn't matter. In fact, it makes what you did even better." He studied her. She looked weary. "You're tired. I'll take you home."

A light rain began falling just as the couple walked down the front steps of the mercantile. Ivy shivered.

"Here." Baxter took off his jacket and placed it gently over her shoulders. Together they ran through the rain.

"Try to get some rest," he urged her when he left her at her door. "You deserve it."

To Ivy's relief, her mother had already gone to bed and fallen asleep. She pulled out her narrow sofa bed. She would explain everything tomorrow.

Even though she was tired, Ivy found it difficult to sleep. Her mind kept reliving the events of the evening. Had God led her into the store and given her the courage even though she didn't know what she would find? Ivy knew she couldn't have done it alone. Someone must have been helping her. And wasn't it odd that she had found Mrs. Fallon, of all people, the woman she hated so?

Ivy appreciated Mrs. Fallon admitting she had accused Ivy falsely. She had to forgive Mrs. Fallon for that. She had learned long ago at the circus that hatred hurts others. It also hurts the person who hates. Paulo's anger over having to keep the Tarantinos' act together had spilled onto her and the others. But it had hurt him the most. He was bitter and mean-spirited. People were afraid to be around him. Ivy had been afraid to be around him. But God had taken care of her through her friends Gyppo and Sophia and Liselle. She wasn't afraid anymore, and she didn't hate Paulo anymore.

Now, in spite of Mrs. Fallon's meanness over the past months, she wasn't going to hate her either. Working at the store had been difficult, but tonight's circumstances had changed everything. Only God could have brought this about. Once again, he had taken care of her, making sure that the truth came to light. He had changed Mrs. Fallon's heart too. It was a miracle.

Rain pounded the shingles on the roof. The memory of hearing rain many years ago surfaced ever so gently in her mind. The memories were hazy. Her papa. Her mama. Something in Ivy's heart ached. Then the picture of riding in the Ellisons' splendid dark green carriage that first day in Brookdale floated across her mind. In spite of Daddy Dan's problems, Ivy loved her parents. They had been good to her. It no longer mattered what other people thought. Truly, God had rescued a young scared orphan and given her a home.

Over and over the events of her life tumbled in Ivy's mind. The feelings of abandonment were ebbing away like the tide. Just then, she heard the distant whistle of the night train coming into the Brookdale station. She smiled. For the first time, she didn't feel sad inside. The sound was so familiar. The feeling of loneliness that it used to bring was beginning to go away.

Through the night shadows, she spotted her tiny black Bible sitting on the end table. Miss Clinock had tucked it into her pocket years ago before she left the orphanage. Ivy realized that God had truly been watching out for her all this time. Surely his goodness and mercy had followed her all the days of her life.

25

The next morning, sunshine flooded the tiny parlor. As Ivy woke up, she heard the kettle whistling in the kitchen. Her mother appeared, dressed and smiling.

"You're awake," she said from the arch of the doorway. "It's almost 7:15. You'll be late for work." As she turned back toward the kitchen, she added, "I made some coffee."

A few moments later, she reappeared with a steaming cup and handed it to Ivy.

"Thanks." Ivy managed a smile and placed the cup on the end table. "Sit down, Mother." She patted the edge of the couch. "I have something to tell you."

When Ivy told her what had happened with Mrs. Fallon, Mercedes was angry. "How could she accuse you like that? That awful woman. And to think I slept through the entire episode!" An expression of pain crossed her face. "Darling, I've let you bear so much alone."

"You didn't know, Mother. How could you? Besides, what could you have done?"

"I could've been stronger all along. Not been such an ostrich, with my head stuck in the sand." She sat up straight. "From now on, things are going to be different."

Mercedes wrapped her arms around her daughter and the two hugged. Tears ran down both their cheeks.

Just before noon, Mercedes put on her blue hat, picked up the shopping basket, and declared, "I'm going to the market to buy groceries for a dinner fit for a queen! You just rest, dear."

Ivy bathed and dressed. As she was brushing her freshly washed hair, she heard a knock at the door. It was Baxter.

"For you," he said, handing her a pot of white hyacinths.

"Thank you." She buried her nose in the fragrant blooms. "Mmmm, delicious! Makes me know spring is coming."

"May I come in? I'd like to talk to you."

"Of course." Ivy stepped back and held the door wider for him. "Would you like a cup of coffee?"

"No, thanks."

Instead of sitting, Baxter paced the tiny room. His expression was serious. "I've been up half the night thinking. There are some things we need to discuss."

Ivy set down the hyacinth on the table and sat down on the couch. "What things?" she wondered aloud.

"Important things. Us."

"Us?"

Baxter kept pacing back and forth. "I've spent a lot of time thinking about us, Ivy. About what happened to us. I was angry when you got engaged, I admit." Baxter stopped in mid sentence. "I know you blame me for what happened to your father—"

"I told you," she interrupted. "I don't blame you anymore. My father has admitted his mistakes."

Baxter was silent for a few moments. He stopped walking and turned to face her. "I love you, Ivy," he said softly.

"I've never stopped loving you. What I have to find out is how you feel about me. Could you love me again?"

Ivy looked at him. "There are things you don't know about me. Things about my past that no one in Brookdale knows. I've never told anyone. I've been afraid people wouldn't accept me if they knew. Even coming here on the Orphan Train is something I've wanted to forget."

"Do you think any of that matters to me? I don't care about the past. I know you now, and I love you just as you are."

"Sit down," Ivy urged. "I need to tell you one thing I did that changed my life and Allison's too. I never even told Allison until right before she got married."

Baxter was frowning. He sat down beside her. Ivy began her long story starting with the night she learned her papa had been killed. She told him about the circus and St. Luke's Hospital. She related how she had exchanged dresses with Allison on the Orphan Train.

"So you see, I'm not the admirable person you think I am. I'm a fraud."

Baxter grabbed her hands. "Don't be so hard on yourself, Ivy. You're talking about an eight-year-old child. No one can blame you for what you did." He held them tighter. "Just think of all you survived before you were even ten years old! The death of your parents, the circus, being adopted by strangers. Not many people would have had what it takes to survive all that. That's courage, Ivy."

"Baxter, Mother and Daddy don't even know about me trading dresses with Allison."

He squeezed her hands. "You've made the Ellisons very happy. That's all that matters." Baxter leaned toward her. "Nobody can do anything about the past, Ivy. It's gone. But we can plan for the future. I love you, and I want to marry you. Will you marry me?"

Ivy did not answer him right away. Tears crowded her eyes. "Baxter, I can't leave Mother until Daddy comes home."

"I'm not asking you to. Let me share the responsibility with you. You've struggled on your own long enough. You don't have to go it alone anymore." He grinned. "Doesn't the Bible say that two are better than one?"

Ivy had to laugh.

"So, what's the answer? Will you at least consider marrying me?"

Just then, the parlor door opened and Mercedes walked in.

Baxter jumped to his feet. "Good morning, Mrs. Ellison. I've just proposed to your daughter. I'd like to ask you for her hand in marriage."

Mercedes held the groceries in her arms. "Nothing could make me happier, Baxter. I know Dan would agree."

Ivy was stunned. Things were happening too fast. Baxter and her mother were both beaming at her.

Ivy suddenly remembered the long loneliness of her life. As she looked at the two of them, she considered what her life might be like if she gave Baxter the answer he wanted. She would have someone who would love and cherish her. Someone to support her. A home, children. Baxter McNeil was standing there, offering her everything she had ever yearned for. And she did love him. She knew that now. She felt peace. Something wonderful was happening.

She nodded her head. "Yes," she replied.

Instantly, Baxter stepped forward and drew her up into his arms. Ivy closed her eyes for his kiss.

Yes, it was true. Her life was in God's hands. And just like Liselle had said, God was taking care of the rest.

About the Author

I grew up in a small Southern town, in a home of storytellers and readers, where authors were admired and books were treasured and discussed. When I was nine years old, an accident confined me to bed. As my body healed, I spent hours at a time making up stories for my paper dolls to act out. That is when I began to write stories.

As a young woman, three books had an enormous impact on me: *Magnificent Obsession, The Robe,* and *Christy.* From these novels I learned that stories held the possibility of changing lives. I wanted to learn to write books with unforgettable characters who faced choices and challenges and were so real that they lingered in readers' minds long after they finished the book.

The Orphan Train West for Young Adults series is especially dear to my heart. I first heard about these orphans when I read an *American Heritage* magazine story titled "The Children's Migration." The article told of the orphan trains taking more than 250,000 abandoned children cross country to be placed in rural homes. I knew I had to write some of their stories. Toddy, Laurel, Kit, Ivy and Allison, and April and May are all special to me. I hope you will grow to love them as much as I do.

Jane Peart lives in Fortuna, California, with her husband, Ray.

The Orphan Train West for Young Adults Series

They seek love with new families . . . and turn to God to find ultimate happiness.

The Orphan Train West for Young Adults series provides a glimpse into a fascinating and little-known chapter of American history. Based on the actual history of hundreds of orphans brought by train to be adopted by families in America's heartland, this delightful series will capture your heart and imagination.

Popular author Jane Peart brings the past to life with these heartwarming novels set in the 1800s, which trace the lives of courageous young girls who are searching for fresh beginnings and loving families. As the girls search for their purpose in life, they find strength in God's unconditional love.

Follow the girls' stories as they pursue their dreams, find love, grow in their faith, and move beyond the sorrows of the past.

Look for the other books in the Orphan Train West for Young Adults series!

TODDY

JANE PEART

Toddy

Orphan Train West SERIES

Left at Boston's Greystone Orphanage by her actress mother, exuberant Toddy sets out on the Orphan Train along with her two friends, Kit and Laurel. On the way, the three make a pact to stay "forever friends." When they reach the town of Meadowridge, Toddy joins the household of Olivia Hale, a wealthy widow who wants a companion for her delicate granddaughter, Helene. Before long, Toddy wins their hearts and brightens their home with her optimism and zest for life.

As the years pass, Toddy brings much joy to Helene and Mrs. Hale. Yet happiness eludes her. Is Toddy's yearning for a home only a dream?

LAUREL

Shy, sensitive Laurel is placed at Boston's Greystone Orphanage when her mother enters a sanitarium. After her mother's death, Laurel is placed on the Orphan Train with Kit and Toddy, destined for the town of Meadowridge. There she is adopted by Dr. and Mrs. Woodward, who still grieve for the daughter they lost two years earlier.

Laurel brings a breath of fresh air— and much love—into the Woodwards' home. As she grows up, though, Laurel longs to discover her true identity. Her search leads her to Boston, where she uncovers secrets from her past. But will Laurel's new life come between her and the love she desires?

KIT

After her grieving, widowed father leaves Kit, her younger brother, and her baby sister at Greystone Orphanage in Boston, Kit wants desperately to bring the family back together. But the younger children are adopted and Kit is sent West on the Orphan Train. Along the way, she and her friends, Toddy and Laurel, make a pact to be "forever friends." At the end of their journey, they each go to live with different families in the town of Meadowridge.

Kit is taken by the Hansens, a farm family who wants to adopt a girl to help the weary mother of five boys. Kit rises above her dreary situation by excelling in her schoolwork. But will she ever realize her secret longings to love and be loved?

JANE PEART

Kit

Orphan Train West
SERIES